TARA AND SANDY

Slow Dance of Infinite Stars

Sita Bhaskar & Sabarna Roy

Leadstart
INKSTATE

ISBN
Hardcase: 978-93-5610-844-8
Paperback: 978-93-5610-845-5

First published in India 2022 by Leadstart Inkstate
A brand of One Point Six Technologies Pvt. Ltd.

123, Building J2, Shram Seva Premises,
Wadala Truck Terminal,
Mumbai 400022, Maharashtra, INDIA
Phone: +91 96999 33000
Email: info@leadstartcorp.com
www.leadstartcorp.com

Disclaimer: This is a work of fiction. All the names, characters, businesses, places, events and incidents in this book are either the product of the author's imagination or used in a fictitious manner. Any resemblance to actual persons, living or dead, or actual events is purely coincidental.

Editor: Shayoni Mitra
Cover: Maharaja R
Layouts: Sathish Kumar

To all the friends in our lives

Anyone who falls in love is searching for the missing pieces of themselves. So anyone who's in love gets sad when they think of their lover. It's like stepping back inside a room you have fond memories of, one you haven't seen in a long time.

– Haruki Murakami

Also by Sita Bhaskar

Flirting With Trouble
Shielding Her Modesty

Also by Sabarna Roy

Literary Works:

Pentacles
Frosted Glass
Abyss
Winter Poems
Random Subterranean Mosaic:
2012–2018 Time Frozen in Myriad Thoughts
Etchings of the First Quarter of 2020
Fractured Mosaic
A Marriage, An Affair, and A Friendship

Technical Works:

Articles on Ductile Iron Pipelines and Framework Agreement
Methodology
Technological Trends in Water Sector for a Sustainable Solution
Emerging Environmental Technologies and Policies

Sita Bhaskar is the author of two books: *Flirting with Trouble* and *Shielding Her Modesty*.

She is a contributor to *The Oldest Love Story: A Motherhood Anthology*, and to *In the Silence of this Room* – listed as a novel semi-finalist in 2008 William Faulkner Creative Writing Competition (and later published by Grey Sparrow Press).

While her short stories have been published in several literary magazines, her short story, *Swayamvaram*, which appeared in Crab Orchard Review's special issue, *Come Together – Occasions, Ceremonies & Celebrations*, was listed in Best American Short Stories (BASS) under '100 other distinguished stories.'

Photo Credit: Suman Saha

Sabarna Roy is Senior Vice President [Business Development] at Electrosteel Castings Limited, an author of eight Literary and three Technical bestselling books, TEDx Speaker, Champions of Change Award 2020 Winner, Times Excellence Award 2021 Winner in Indian Literature, and Golden Glory Award Winner for Critically Acclaimed Bestselling Author of the Year 2021.

Sabarna Roy has been awarded the Right Choice Award for Author of Eminence of 2022. He has been selected among the India Today Group: Icons of India.

Roy has also received the Best Author to Watch 2022 Award from Indo-Global Entrepreneurship Conclave Delhi organized by Business Connect, and Best Author in Indian English Literature of 2022 at the Ninth Asia Education Summit 2022.

Sabarna Roy has received a letter of confirmation from Confederation of International Accreditation Commission [CIAC] Global Foundation stating that he will be receiving an Honorary Doctor of Arts, Honoris Causa from Azteca University, Mexico.

Contents

Foreword

Letter writing is dead... conversation is a lost art... so wails the chorused lament in the time of the now redundant SMS, lazy WhatsApp forwards, short emails and shorter Twitter posts. The lament is also for language mauled by truncated spellings and newly minted abbreviations. Most opportunely comes *Tara and Sandy: Slow Dance of Infinite Stars,* an irreverent novel that revives both letter writing and intelligent conversation in a compelling narrative. It is a narrative that has room for arbitrary digressions, throwaway asides and awkward reticence that is appealing in its ungainliness. This adds texture to letters from people who are starting out afresh after a hiatus of 30 odd years. The letters between Sandy and Tara speak in voices that are very different and eloquent in their own distinct way. Catching up with well-lived lives after school days reminiscences, the words kindle a suggestive slow burn that soon crackles with sexual chemistry. Two lonely adults seeking a connection that could ripen with possibilities.

The archaic epistolary novel that was born in the 18th century is reimagined and made provocatively contemporary: lively exploration of the past without nostalgia, and living in and for the moment. The raison d'être of the epistolary form was to convey immediacy along with insights into the mind of the characters. It became a rage in England and Europe. Samuel Richardson's *Pamela* and *Clarissa* are classics in this genre. Goethe's *The Sorrows of Young Werther* haloes the new genre with gravitas. Leap a century and more... Bram Stoker's *Dracula* uses information like news clippings and letters to heighten suspense; readers know more than the characters and wait for the denouement with bated breath. More recently, *Bridget Jones Diary* and the rom com blockbuster *You've Got Mail* recast a freewheeling form into successful movies.

In one sense, *Tara and Sandy: Slow Dance of Infinite Stars* adheres to the classic definition of an epistolary novel. The form may be classic, but the spirit is as modern as tomorrow! This slim novel doesn't hurl us into immediacy for its own sake. It leads us to this sense of urgency as two schoolmates, not exactly great friends, resume a long-distance relationship in a desultory fashion after a chance meeting at an airport – a standard meet cute cliché. Sandy and Tara positively reject the *meet cute* formula. After twelve long years, Sandy takes the initiative with a long ballad dedicated to Tara and her answer is amused, intrigued and non-committal.

This slow dance of advance and retreat proceeds like a Tango in suspension, arrested mid-movement. Sandy is more forthcoming with his amatory past, his serial infidelities interspersed with bits of poetry (his own and Pushkin on one occasion) and jottings from his journal. Sandy's letters live up to the dictionary meaning of epistolary: it could include quotations, other documents and such. Tara is upfront but willing to indulge Sandy's meandering missives embedded with covert hints. Tara's letters cut with sarcasm but are also vivid with imagery as befits a filmmaker who has abandoned her profession. When she writes of an accident while shooting in freezing Canadian winter, we see it happen. What could be dissonance of tones in their letters lends an edge of uncertainty that keeps us guessing.

So begins this promising but often dilatory letter-writing between two adults well past their prime, carrying the luggage of relationships that failed (Sandy), reconciled to three serious relationships that had ended (Tara). Their letters glide from the personal anecdote to philosophical questioning, from nostalgia to the airing of grievances. Sandy and Tara come alive through their conversations as a man and a woman who embark on a relationship through words… words that carry the weight of memories, inarticulate longing, sharp comebacks and the tantalising promise of something more.

It is not surprising that Tara is a trained filmmaker. Cinema reinvented the epistolary form after the novel lost its initial novelty. It was parodied in its rather lengthy lifetime. Now it remains a curiosity, except for English literature students looking for an old peg to hang their new theses. Films like *The Blair Witch Project* and the *Paranormal Activity* franchise use "found footage" and home videos to give authenticity to imagined stories. Novels now use cinematic tropes and insert emails, texts and power point presentations for staccato tempo. Tara's sharp observations power the letters with humour and matter-of-fact brevity. The alternating rhythms and tempo of the narrative keep us riveted. Since I am a film critic and digressed to films, let me paraphrase a classic line from *All about Eve*. Fasten your hold on the book. We are in for a rocky, disruptive ride.

Maithili Rao
6th June 2022

Maithili Rao is a film critic and the author of *Smita Patil: A Brief Incandescence*. Her new book *Millennial Women in Bollywood: A New Brand* is due for publication in 2022.

Before

TARA

Tara used to be my schoolmate;
I met her twenty-six years after we had left school.

It's not as if I remembered her very often;
But if I reminisced on my school days,
Her face quivered in the frame of my subconscious,
Somewhere in its left bottom quadrant.
Well, what made her worth remembering were her large moist eyes,
Her beautiful black hair tied in a well-knotted bun,
Her well-developed bosoms and her strong legs.

She was the daughter of our music teacher;
Tara played the tunes of Beatles songs on the piano,
This made her an enigma in school.

I can tell you: There are two kinds of beauties on this planet…
One, who lose their beauty to age, and another, who ripen with time.
The former makes me immensely sad;
While the latter, happy and strangely envious.

When I came across Tara after so many years at the Delhi airport,
She was slowly munching a sweetened butterfly biscuit,
And washing her snack with sips of steaming black coffee.

I did not recognize her at first. She looked swollen, her hair was
coloured,
And her legs were covered by a long maroon skirt.
But the eyes were unmistakably melancholic,
As they used to be in the adolescent years,
Finally, when we met, the house was on fire!
We looked for comfortable places in a lounge café,
As if we had all the time in the world for each other.
For some time, we chit-chatted avoiding the core of our lives.
The lager that we drank must have created a spectre in our souls,
I found the pieces of our conversation dangling,
On the periphery of a dangerous jungle.

Tara said with a sparkling smile on her lips:
Sandy, you've aged; you no longer look that handsome!
The image from school that I carry in my mind,
You need not sulk, for I've aged too and I know I look ugly!
No, she was neither fishing for compliments nor sad about what
she said;
She was plainly speaking facts: I could realize that.
You know what, Sandy: I migrated to Canada after high school,
With flickering dreams in my eyes,
Did my graduation from a film-school in Montreal,
My life is a whirlwind!

I tried to make a film on a story about a girl,
Who was locked up in a dungeon,
For the first eighteen years of her life by her crazy father.
And when she comes out of it she is in a stupor;
She fails to communicate with the outside world,
not knowing their language.

Let me tell you Sandy:
Silence is the pinnacle of isolation; it kills us from inside…

When you have been abandoned by the soul that you love most
dearly,
You plunge into absolute isolation and absolute silence,
Like the few moments before you die.

In the last twenty years I have loved a Frenchman, a Swede and a
Mexican;
I was dumped by all of them in the end.
Each time I had to crawl up an abyss,
Similar to an unending shaft of a coal mine:
Breathless and infinitely depressed.

I lost my child in the eighth month succumbing to a sudden fall,
While on a shoot across a snow-covered meadow.
How many bridges can you cross, my dear; tell me about you
Sandy;
I have been a pathetic chatterbox truly.

I did not know what to say to Tara.
I felt embarrassed to talk about the life of a seasoned bureaucrat,
Who constantly makes deals and money on the sly.
Sitting opposite Tara and hearing the story of her intense life,
I felt a pain rising up in my body like a fountain of light.
I realized, I have spent a shallow life,
I felt humbled.

We kept the conversation going,
I asked her: Have you come back now?
She said: I wish to settle down in Pondicherry by the sea.
Why did you come back, Tara?
She replied to my query looking in my eyes:
I wanted to migrate to a land of opportunities, Sandy; to a country
That was not hesitant to nurture unconventional pursuits;
Most of all I hated the heat, dust and humidity of our places,

And the festering wounds of impoverishment everywhere,
But when I lost hope of survival in a foreign land,
And the moral strength to continue in absolute darkness,
That comes with the frenzy of silence and isolation,
It was my land (to whose air, food and language I belonged)
That beckoned me in my dreams sending me streams of light and warmth,
(Embracing me in its delicate haze) as if telling me softly,
I could survive here with a chance.

We kept quiet for a long time.
Then our planes were announced, and we departed silently.

Reaching home, I told the story of Tara to my wife.
She looked worried and her look was asking me:
Were you in love with Tara in school?
Since my wife is intelligent and knows all the tricks of riddled conversation,
She asked me nothing.

After midnight, locked in our arms, I told her this:
You know darling; we had a definition of happiness in school.
What?
Happy will that man be whom Tara would marry!
My wife whispered in my ears:
But she herself was such an unhappy woman,
And she married no one and so my darling Sandy,
You still have a chance to be happy with her.

I got up, held my wife in my arms in a strong embrace,
And made love slowly almost cherishing each moment,

Like it was my only residual lifespan,
Under the gaze of million stars blazing against a brilliant sky.

2009
Kolkata

After

January 4th, 2022
Kolkata

Dear Tara,

We met at the Delhi Airport in 2009, twenty-six years after we left school. When I returned to Kolkata, I wrote a ballad on you that was published in my first book, Pentacles. I gifted the ballad to you. While you mentioned it was an extraordinary gesture, you did not comment on the qualities of the ballad. Which I took for your not liking the ballad very much.

We exchanged our numbers and contact details, but we hardly kept in touch. Of course, this could be because we were fighting personal battles in our own war zones. In 2019, the Covid pandemic crushed us to remoteness.

A few days back, I was going through my old papers when I chanced upon your details. I thought of sending an e-mail to you! If you are okay, you will reply. Possibly...

I lost my mother in 2009. My father is still alive and kicking at the age of eighty-six.

I am on my second marriage. I have a daughter from my wife's first husband and a son from my first wife. My son lives in London. Both my children are doing well. They have their own interests, and they have moved away from me.

My wife is the Headmistress in an underprivileged school, and she is doing great!

In 2011, I was afflicted by a major bout of depression. Since then, I have been on anti-depressants and anti-anxiety pills. They have done wonders to my nervous system. They have taken away the fear of anything in life.

Why am I continuing with the anti-depressants and anti-anxiety pills even today? Simply put, I do not have the balls to face another bout of depression. There is no clear-cut answer to why I went into a depression, except that melancholia has been an invisible and silent friend all my life.

One of the critical things that has happened in the last two years is that my interest in women has gone down, and this, I find pretty morbid. It is like losing interest in life.

I am not unwell, but I do not feel very well either. It does not have anything to do with fear of death. In my present state of mind, I do not fear death. Although, strangely, at the same time, I crave to die in my sleep.

I am worried though, that I may soon get partially dysfunctional...

Hold on, I am not trying to unburden my illnesses on your mindscape. I am just trying to say how I am now.

My concentration is very scattered at the present moment. I cannot read very fat books or watch very long TV series or movies, which until a few years back I used to do with great enthusiasm and interest.

I am losing my capacity to talk. After writing eleven books, I am afraid, writing a sentence bores me to death. So, I thought let me try writing a letter to you.

The most worrisome part is: my wife, my children, my father, and the people at work want me to be a super functional and operational person all the time; but clearly, I am not. And I am not able to communicate with them that I am not! My worry is, they will unnecessarily worry about me! I do not want them to worry about me.

But not telling my situation to anybody is putting me inside a cage. A cage from which I cannot come out.

I think the real sickness that saddles me is that I have been so used to comforts in life, and add-on privileges, that I make no effort to lead a natural life. I am running out of the first-hand experiences in life.

I live inside a rat hole, although from the outside it looks like an opulent home.

I am no longer restless. I enjoy sitting in my armchair looking at photo albums, and art books. I love listening to Coldplay and Hooverphonic.

A few days back, a photograph of my parents worried me a lot.

In this photograph, my mother is looking obliquely at my father, and my father is looking at the camera. Somehow, when I look at it, I feel my mother wants the attention of my father but is not getting it. The photograph made me very sad. I listened to Hooverphonic's Mad About You to lift up my mood. It did lift my mood somewhat, but the sadness did not go away.

My sister is nine years younger to me. Before my sister was born, my mother would kiss me a lot. She stopped kissing me completely after my sister was born.

If you reply to me, I will invite you to Kolkata. Kolkata has many beautiful parks now - full of flowers, water bodies, and breeze. It's nice taking a stroll in the parks and gardens, and having some conversation and may be some chocolates. Sadly, I am diabetic and hypertensive. So you can have all the chocolates.

No more of me.

Bye bye,

Love,
Sandy

January 20th, 2022
Pondicherry

Hi Sandy,

A voice from the past! Has it really been more than a dozen years since we met at the airport?

They say *time flies when you are having fun*. I think it should be *time flies when you are getting old*, though you seem to have specific wishes on how you want to leave this world. In your sleep? I don't care how I die, as long as it is quick – like a *candle in the wind* to quote Elton John – did he write the lyrics? Or was he the singer? It was all so long ago.

But I digress.

Did I not comment on the ballad you wrote about me? Maybe it was because I was not used to anyone writing anything in my honour (or should that be *memory*?). Anyway, after receiving your mail, I got a copy of *Pentacles* to read the ballad again. Thank you. I would say you have encapsulated my memory of the encounter at the airport, though I am not sure what you meant by saying I looked *swollen*. Water retention after a long flight? Lack of makeup? Puffy eyes? Swollen feet? I had just arrived on a transatlantic flight and was waiting for my connecting flight to Pondicherry. That is my excuse for looking 'swollen' and I'm sticking to it!

While I am sorry to hear about your bout with anxiety and depression a couple of years after we met, it looks like you have learned to live with it, by feeding it adequate doses of anti-depressants and anti-anxiety meds. But this constant war against oneself – performing at an optimal level at work and at home – does get tiring and exhausting, doesn't it? Sometimes one goes to work to get away from the anxiety-filled eyes at home, and at other times, one wants to come back home to get away from the *be your best* atmosphere at work.

Where can one go to be by yourself? Into your head, I guess. And that starts the cycle all over again!

Thank you for sharing the details of your family. I don't have any family updates to give you besides what I told you at the airport. No additional relationships and no unexpected children to speak of. I didn't realize you were on your second marriage. Did I forget or were you on your first marriage when we met? And if you were – this is kinda awkward – so I'll leave it here – for you to answer (or not!)

I did notice the heavy heart with which you say you have lost interest in women in the last two years. Two years? The pandemic years? Well, it has been an unsettling time of our lives, don't you think? So much uncertainty, so much anguish, so much heartbreak. I'm no sexologist – is that what they call them? – but could it be because of that? Actually, that is not a question to which I need an answer. I'm merely throwing out a probable cause.

But not being able to read a book or write a story – ah, now that is something I would definitely worry about. What do you do instead of that? That is, with the time you used to spend on these activities? Have you filled it up with other interests? Art books, music – yes, that would help. But photo albums?

I find photo albums morbid. So many what-ifs in photos. So many photographic triggers of how things were, and nostalgia of wanting to go back to that time or re-living the past with horror. Depends, I suppose, on what happened.

I mean, look at you – trying to analyze a photograph of your mother and father. Did you feel he didn't give her enough attention? Or now that she is gone and he is eighty-six, he feels he did not give her the attention she needed? Or is this you regretting that after your sister was born, you didn't get the attention you deserved? See, that is the problem with photo albums. You wander through the lanes of memory stumbling down paths you have forgotten and don't know your way back from. That is why I dread photo albums.

Have I pretty much taken every sentence of your correspondence and turned it around on its head? I'm sorry – this is what I do. So, think long and hard before you say, 'If you reply to me…'

At my end, things have been jogging along at a pace that I enjoy. I have made Pondicherry my base, and life here satisfies me to the extent that I could almost be content living here. I have been travelling off and on, but mostly for work. Not work for any client, but work for myself – using my film school education to make pieces that I think will dazzle the world with its brilliance, should I choose to display it in the right forums. We all have our fantasies, I guess!

So here goes – I did reply. This feels like homework. If you remember, back in high school, I was one of those who never did their homework. There were a lot of goody-two-shoes guys like you who would allow me to copy from you. I suppose I carried that desultory attitude into adulthood, which is why I wander through life doing a little bit of this and a little bit of that!

Before I give away the entire plot, I will stop and retreat while the going is good.

Take care,
Tara

January 21st, 2022
Kolkata

Dear Tara,

Now that you have replied to me, I send you my formal invitation to visit Kolkata.

The songwriters of *Candle In The Wind* are Bernie Taupin and Elton John. This is a song, which I also like very much. Possibly, I would have listened to this song more than 250 times. You may be aware that the song was originally written in 1973, in honour of Marilyn Monroe, who had died 11 years earlier. In 1997, John performed a rewritten version of the song, *Candle In The Wind 1997*, as a tribute to Diana, Princess of Wales.

I have visited Pondicherry six times - two times on professional work, once for leisure, and three times for book reading sessions. It is a mystery that in my six visits to Pondicherry, in a small place like that, I never bumped into you. My walks along the road on the seafront have been memorable.

One of the critical things that has happened to me during the pandemic years is that I have lost my appetite for travelling to distant places. This year, possibly during summer, I will be travelling to London to visit my son. He wants to take us to the Scottish Highlands. During the winter, my son is planning to arrange a trip for us to Kochi and Kumarakom, the two places I loved to visit again and again once upon a time.

You may find my photo albums morbid, but I think they rekindle the magical memories of the past. It is significantly different from what we know as nostalgia.

A few years back, I wrote a tiny piece in my journal about Kochi that I reproduce here for you to read. It goes as follows:

Last night I dreamt of the colossal fishing nets of Kochi; the way I had seen them for the first time in my life in 2003 against the backdrop of an orangish, glowing and melting, and yet a setting sun. Later I visited Kochi in 2004 and 2006. I have always desired Satyajit Ray to set a Feluda mystery in Kochi during the early 1970s when he was writing in his prime.

Serene Kochi has been drawing traders and explorers to its shores for over 600 years. Nowhere else in India will you find such an intriguing mix: giant fishing nets from China, a 400-year-old synagogue, ancient mosques, Portuguese houses, and the crumbling remains of the British Raj. The result is an unlikely blend of medieval Portugal, Holland, and an English village grafted onto the tropical Malabar Coast. It's a delightful place to spend some time and nap in some of India's finest homestays and heritage accommodations. Kochi is also a centre for Keralan arts and one of the best places to see Kathakali and Kalarippayattu.

Mainland Ernakulam is the hectic transport and cosmopolitan hub of Kochi, while the historical towns of Fort Cochin and Mattancherry, though well-touristed, remain wonderfully atmospheric- thick with the smell of the past. Other islands, including Willingdon and Vypeen, are linked by a network of ferries and bridges.

In 2004, I had visited Kumarakom for the first time, and I wrote a tiny piece in my journal, titled: *Vembanad*

Lake, which was reproduced in my fifth book, *Random Subterranean Mosaic: 2012 - 2018*, and it is reproduced below for you to read:

Lakes of Desire: In 2004 we visited Kerala and spent a lot of our time at The Taj Kumarakom Lake Resort situated by the side of Vembanad Lake. Kerala has a number of such lakes. The first and foremost is the green algae-rich Vembanad lake 15 km from Kottayam (Kumarakom). It is the longest lake in India. It is part of an extensive wetland system with the largest source of surface water. A number of rivers flow into the lake making it deep and vast.

The lake is divided into two halves by a saltwater barrier and you can see the difference between the brackish and fresh water. It was constructed to prevent the intrusion of sea water. Just cruising along the lake can make your trip worthwhile, as you can see parts of three districts which surround the lake.

The bird sanctuary can also be seen nearby; the sanctuary is home to various migratory birds from all over the world. The serene lake comes alive during Onam with a spectacular water regatta - the snake boat races. It is indeed amazing to watch oarsmen, at least a hundred in one boat, slice their way through the waters to the fast rhythm of their own full-throated singing.

We spent three complete days exploring the length and breadth of the lake from morning till afternoon on a two-tiered boat exclusively hired for us.

In the backdrop of Pondicherry, I have written a tiny story, titled: *Mari Esai* in my fifth book, as well, which is reproduced below for you to read:

Mari Esai (I am borrowing the name of the protagonist of After Dark by Haruki Murakami to camouflage the real person) is a Japanese girl, around 25 years, living in Pondicherry. She is an artist. She has a small shop near the Goubert Market where she displays her artworks – watercolours, charcoal sketches, small paintings in pastel colours, and pencil sketches. She is very good at Indian countryside landscapes, faces of aged farmers, and fishermen, elephants, leopards, and lonely moonlit oceans. She has travelled through the Indian heartland with her French stepfather who introduced her to painting. Her Japanese parents came to settle in Pondicherry when she was two years old and separated when she was ten years old, after which her mother married her French stepfather. Her shop is visited by locals and tourists alike. People like to have a view of her minimalist (although arresting enough) works, and her working live, in a corner of her shop, which is also a good place to have joints and hookah – provisions for which are made by her. Mari's father – short and stout with Samurai features – is a skilled kick-boxer (which he has now abandoned), and a sharp businessman dealing in exotic Japanese artefacts. Gradually he turned to drinking. But he is popular with women. Earlier he had a violent temper and suffered sudden mood swings. Mari's stepfather is an Indologist. He has beautiful blue eyes, silky hair, and is a foot, and a half taller than her (and her mother). Mari's father did not leave Pondicherry because of Mari. He wanted to spend some time with Mari every other day. This is what he had negotiated with Mari's mother at the time of separation. Mari's stepfather introduced her to a world of ideas – especially around the civilization of the subcontinent – and arts including calligraphy. Mari's father's love is raw and obsessive; he is extremely jealous of Mari's stepfather even after so many years. Mari's stepfather's love never feels like love because it is so refined and prim and proper yet he is curious about Mari's life in his own careful way (although in reality, he is possessive about her); Mari suspects that her stepfather is also secretly jealous of her father. These two men are fighting an invisible battle through Mari over Mari. Mari always feels a surge of love for her father. Mari feels a sense of indebtedness to her stepfather for teaching her so many new things and treating her mother with love and care. Mari is so torn between these two men that she has no space left in her heart for a lover who desires her for her looks and essence. So Mari continuously keeps on working on her art.

Actually, looking at old photographs of mine, and the growing up years of my children secretly intertwined with my own life is an exhilarating experience.

Why has friendship between men and women been so rare and difficult? The usual answer is sex. But this forgets that friendship between men has not been easy either. The very first friendship of which there is a historical record, between the Babylonians Gilgamesh and Elkidu, around 2000 BC, immediately ran into trouble, because their temperaments were too different. Elkidu was a 'wild man'. They had to negotiate before they eventually agreed to set off together 'to rid the world of evil'. It was not sex that thwarted friendship, so much as fear of people who are different.

I am worried about my own life.

The point is: although I feel angry at instances of gross abuse of institutional power, I do nothing to resist them effectively. Rather, I am shrouded by a cloud of evil hopelessness and make a confusion of my own life and the circumstances occurring all around. I ponder why is it that my intellectual self has no control over my ethical self to chart a course that is less manipulative of people and circumstances. Sometimes I feel my body is trapped inside my evil soul and at other times, I feel my soul is caged inside my hedonistic body.

Do reply.

Bye bye,

Love,
Sandy

January 29th, 2022
Pondicherry

Hi Sandy,

The longer one lives, the more items go into the *I did not know that* category.

I did not know that *Candle in the Wind* was written for Marilyn Monroe. I had always attributed it to Elton John's tribute to Lady Diana. But it could be argued that both women were candles in the wind.

For me, Marilyn Monroe is a legend only because of hearsay – she was before my time. That said, about ten years ago I happened to visit Chicago when a giant structure of Monroe's iconic image was installed as part of an art project on the Magnificent Mile section of downtown Chicago. You know the image? In a white dress over the subway grate? From Billy Wilder's *The Seven Year Itch.*

My travel companion was entranced by the statue. He confessed to me that, growing up, he had a poster of this pose that took up half the wall space by his bed, so that he could go to sleep looking up her skirt. "You, and half the teenagers in America," I said, and shrugged off his comment. Yes, I was travelling with an older man, and I remember we broke up soon after that incident. Not because of what he said. I'm no prude. To be fair, we had not come to Chicago to see this monument. Didn't even know it was there until we came upon it while walking to the Chicago Tribune office. We were doing a project together and had come to meet some *interested parties*, as we say in India.

While he stood in awed reverie, I spent a lot of time going around the statue and inspecting it from various photographic angles. I watched people taking pictures. Strangely enough, the older men and women were standing in front of the statue: their faces displayed a worshipful reverence as if they were in the divine presence of a Goddess. On the other side of the statue, it was the youngsters who stood between her legs, gazing up her skirt. I guess, in a way, they weren't too different from their fathers, except that they were born in an era where you didn't have to hide what you were looking at. You could even take pictures!

What did I think about the statue? It was more of an anthropological study for me. I was thinking *Fruit of the Loom* or *Hanes* advertisement. Her underclothes, which caused a gasp of adoration and blissful contemplation back in the day, would be called very sensible no-nonsense *granny pants* these days. Not the minuscule wisps of lace with an inadequate cover that we try to pass off as underwear these days. Each era has its markers on what titivates the collective imagination of a population. These days, especially in India, it is the bare quivering waist and thrusting hip that are the equivalent of *looking up her skirt*. To each era, it's own.

Now, why did I go from *Candle in the Wind* to *Quivering in the Wind*? I have no idea. I was going to launch into another detour about Lady D, but I'll hold that off for another day! Let me respond to other parts of your letter.

No, wait. Why wait for another day? What is going to change in my thoughts? Might as well get it all out. Let it all hang out, as they say in America.

While Marilyn Monroe was before my time, Lady D was definitely during my time. I don't know what it was with us in our younger days that we devoured every news tidbit about her – right from the time of her engagement. Her pictures in magazines were highly coveted.

We made deals with the magazine circulating library guy to slip us those magazines first. Was it a colonial hangover? Or just young romantic minds? Who knows! Who even remembers!

While we were older during that soap-opera marriage of hers and had more experience with failing relationships in our own lives to take it in stride, there was a twinge of sadness and regret at a life cut short when she died in that horrendous car accident in Paris. At the same time there was relief that our relationships did not have to suffer from public scrutiny (it was the victim of our own bungling!) and our joys and sorrows were experienced in the privacy of our own social circles rather than being played out in the international media. Our wombs belonged to us, and not to the royal baby-making machine.

I just realized that I've used *we* in the previous para. Rather than go back and correct it, I'll leave it as it is for two reasons: I was after all talking about royalty, so it was appropriate to use the royal *we*! Second reason: I am sure that many of the young girls who were our common classmates in school, would also agree with my thoughts as adults. So, *we* includes all of them.

There. I have transitioned from *we* to *I* and I can continue to the next topic. Or should I call it rebuttal, since I seem to take your letter and address every utterance point by point!

Thank you for sharing pieces of your other writing with me, especially the travel pieces. Sometimes I get so comfortable in my status quo that I am content reading travel blogs and transporting myself to that place in my imagination. I'm all *travelled out* as they say. Did a lot of it in my line of work – film making, in case you don't remember. Now I've become like a doctor in retirement – one who does not want to be reminded that they are a doctor.

Kochi. The one thing I do remember about filming in Kochi was that it was easier and quicker to get permission to film. Ah yes. It takes you to Satyajit Ray and Feluda. Your description takes me back to the Kochi I had forgotten. More recently I remember the BBC documentary series *The Real Marigold Hotel* that had its second season set in Kochi. A bunch of seniors (British, I think) scoping out places to retire. I am happy with my choice of Pondicherry. But I should go back and watch the series again to see if I am tempted to change my mind. Or maybe I should take one more trip to those parts to do the houseboat trip that I've never been on. Like I said, one gets so comfortable with the status quo!

Your comment about fishing nets and setting sun brought to mind an old film that I loved. *Chemmeen.* That film evoked so much lush, earthy, sexual yearnings, without the melodrama you see these days. I remember writing a paper on it in film school.

Your story about *Mari Esai* is very interesting. A young lady cherished by both the father and the stepfather. We should all be so lucky. But the tug of war between the two of them for her love sounds smothering. And the claustrophobic undercurrents it causes has crippled her and left her bereft – to the extent of not having space in her life for a partner of her own. That is sad. I assume she would want that – a partner in her life – in addition to her art.

You have a different premise on the friendships between men and women or even between two men. I assume you are referring to platonic relationships. I don't know if it is the fear of people who are different, or our inability to accept people as they are. In that area, I find women are far better at making and keeping friends, and being there for each other, contrary to common belief. If the toxic serials on television are to be believed, women are brought on earth to make life miserable for other women. That is a very dysfunctional and convoluted commentary on what is in reality an amazing sisterhood of women.

What is this about worrying about your own life? What are you worried about? Your physical safety? Your mental safety? Or is it the helplessness you feel at the gross abuse of institutional power? But your words seem to me more of an internal struggle between what you'd like to be versus what you are, to put it in simple terms. Or is it between what you are versus how you'd like to be perceived? There is a lot of difference between these two perspectives, you know. One, you can fake, the other you can't! Of course, if it is a battle between the good and evil in you, that struggle is as old as the hills, and for each of us, will continue as long as there is breath in our body.

Coming back to the abuse of institutional power, here is my take on it. It may sound a bit jaded, but isn't that what we all are, at this stage of our lives? Each one of us thinks we are born to change the world and we spend the early stages of our independent lives, trying to live up to that ideal. It takes years of throwing our bodies against the wall of indifference to realize that the more you change as a person, the more the world remains the same. Our battles are not something that is fought and done, and we move on to face another one. The same old ones come back at us – like lipstick on a pig – a phrase that is so often used in American politics. For me, that is the part of life that frustrates and angers me. It isn't as if one can sit back and say – there, I've done my part, you don't have to tread the same path again, go forth and fight other battles.

No one generation was born to change the world. It is a constant work-in-progress. I only wish the roots of progress are not pulled out all the time and left to us to re-seed and cultivate yet one more time.

With these rather sombre thoughts, I will release you from this reading!

Take care,
Tara

January 31st, 2022
Kolkata

Dear Tara,

I enjoyed reading your last letter so much that I ended up reading it more than ten times!

But I want to narrate to you two things today. I am feeling very anxious in my mind, and a bit restless and tremulous.

Ashok Babu used to be our neighbour a long time back. He was very close to my mother. He was a clinical schizophrenic. He talked to my mother a lot on the telephone, and confided his life details to her. My mother's name was Debjani, and Ashok Babu told her once that he had a lover during his University days by the name of Debjani, who later two-timed him with his elder brother, and still later cheated on him as well.

Ashok Babu also confided to my mother that he, on two occasions, had witnessed his elder brother having sex with their mother, and they enjoyed their sexual bouts very much. Ashok Babu had said that this was known to his father.

Later, Ashok Babu had an arranged marriage with a woman by the name of Lalita, who was from a very opulent upper-caste home, and Ashok Babu's mother had demanded a lot of dowries, which was given by Lalita's family.

Gradually, Ashok Babu and his wife, Lalita shifted to a separate apartment, which was purchased by Lalita's father. In due course, Ashok Babu's schizophrenia became known to Lalita and her family. Ashok Babu suffered from insomnia, and he would doze off during the day and keep awake at night. He became very sensitive to sounds and sources of light.

His work as a practising scientist at CSIR was adversely affected. Lalita, meanwhile, fell in love with a gym instructor in her neighbourhood, and Ashok Babu spent most of his time in the house alone having switched off the lights and blanked off the windows.

He padded up the spaces below the water taps and showers in the bathrooms as well as the kitchen, with pillows and mattresses so that there would be no sound of water dripping onto the floor.

Ashok Babu would confide to my mother that *they* were coming to kill him. By *they* he meant the consortium of his elder brother, his mother, Lalita, and Lalita's family. He could find traces of their conspiracy littered around everywhere.

Ashok Babu would often go to the nearby markets with ten to fifteen plastic and jute bags in an auto-rickshaw to buy vegetables, groceries, fish and meat, which was cooked by his old aunt-cum-cook, but he rarely ate. He had a huge frame with bulbous eyes and a belly. Children in the neighbourhood feared him. Mysteriously he was attached to my mother, and my mother gave him a patient hearing. Ashok Babu told her about all the conspiracies going on around, and I felt jealous that my mother was giving so much time to this weird man!

My mother used to explain to me that Ashok Babu was a very lonely gentleman, and he needed somebody to talk to. Although he was being treated at a Pavlovian Institute, he seemed to be deteriorating over the years.

Life moved on. I forgot Ashok Babu.

A few days back, a frail, stooping, old man caught me by the side of the tram-car in the portico of City Centre One, and asked me in a wheezing voice: What happened to your mother, Sandy! I had difficulty recognizing the man, but the strangeness of his eyes told me, it was Ashok Babu.

For some reason, I ran away from there in fright and later got to know that Ashok Babu was suffering from Stage-3 pancreatic cancer.

The reason for my anxiety, Tara, is: I realized I did not do the right thing, and last night when I could not sleep, mysteriously, I remembered having written a love letter to you in Standard Ten, which I did not deliver to you in fear of rejection. Like most of the boys in school, I was in love with you. But you did not care much about me because the rumour was, that you never cared much about the studious ones, you liked the guys who were involved in sports and athletics, which I was not into. But very few people knew that I was hooked to listening to cricket commentaries, and my idol of life forever was and is Sunil Manohar Gavaskar.

I tried a lot that night to remember what I had written in that letter. Barely remembered except for the fact that I had reproduced a poem by Pushkin. My mother introduced me to Pushkin.

What does love mean for a teenager? What does love mean for an almost old man like me today? I am very confused.

The *wife* I mentioned in my ballad was actually my lover with whom I was living in, at that time. I was not in a position to marry her because of the acrimonious divorce battle I was engaged with my first wife. My divorce came through early in 2018 and that too successfully because of the intervention of my son. We married legally by the middle of 2018. Having told her about you, and your letters, and my reconnecting with you after so many years she thinks, I love you. Surprisingly, she is neither disturbed by it nor agonized by it. Is it because she may be secretly in love with somebody else!

Is it true that I love you? I am confused about the word. Many years back, I had written: *I believe love is not embedded in duty, responsibility, cause and reason. It is a rage of wind that uproots you from the present, makes your past irrelevant to you and obliterates the significance of a future. Love is happy death.*

Could I capture the essence of love through my words? Because, if this is what love is, I have remained loveless throughout my life. Today, to me, love is the soft incandescence of happiness. Do I feel like that towards you?

Do reply.

Bye bye,

Love,
Sandy

February 6th, 2022
Pondicherry

Hi Sandy,

Whoa now! If you are reading my casual missives more than ten times, I'd better watch out and pay attention to what I write. It is usually in official communications that I am direct but cautious, open yet guarded. Sounds a bit contradictory, I know, but it works.

I am sorry to hear that your mother's friend, Ashok Babu, has stage 3 pancreatic cancer. To have that in addition to mental health issues, specially something like schizophrenia is pretty devastating. But your mother seems to have made a connection with him and she listened to his bizarre stories, which I suspect were the ramblings of his disturbed mind. And in your mother, he found someone to talk to, which was good for him. After all these years, he recognized you enough to ask about her. I know your mother passed away in 2009. Did you tell him about her death before you ran away in fright?

I can see why you are agitated and upset with yourself about having run away from him. Did he bring on reminders about your mother or all the rambling conversations he had with your mother? I hope you get a chance to run into him again so that you can make good on your regrets and lay them to rest.

I'm learning a lot about myself through your recollections, so I hope they are accurate. I was interested in sports jocks back in high school? Seriously? I don't even remember that. I must have lost interest in that subculture because I'm looking around me at this stage of my life – but nope, no sports jocks around.

Sometimes it is good that I don't carry memories from one stage of my life to another. Not because I guard them – so don't think of them as being stacked and locked away in the safe custody of my mind. No. I tend to scatter them behind me like bits of torn paper to be collected into the wastepaper basket of memories and fed into larger garbage bins and hauled off to some landfill of forgotten memories. So, I don't remember the boys back in high school being in love with me. None of them followed me into adulthood, for sure!

Are you still hooked on to cricket commentaries? I lost touch with cricket during my years in Canada, so I'm afraid I have no idols or heroes like Gavaskar to share with you. I did follow basketball for a while but stopped when those Nike shoes that Michael Jordon touted were coveted by teenagers whose parents struggled with two or three jobs to make rent every month. Something about that advertising and jumping up to reach the basket when the people below you were standing on shifting ground did not sit well with me.

We haven't moved far from that dream world, though. Everywhere you see in India, celebrities try to entice you into a lifestyle that is only a pipe dream, and the further you are from reaching it, the more you live in a world of unattainable and unfulfilled desires and urges.

Coming back to sports, I did play co-ed softball for one season with work colleagues in Canada. Not because I wanted to, but because they couldn't get it to be co-ed enough without me, Somehow, only four women agreed to join the team after much persuasion, though there were more women in the office. That should have set off alarms in my mind – to the level of a three-fire alarm! But it was early days in my life in Canada and I wanted to *blend in*. I was the fifth woman. I had no clue how the game was played. Since you remember so much of our high school days, maybe you can tell me if I played any sport or if I just went out with sports jocks!

I was promised that it would be fun, but in my naivete never realized that my work colleagues were intensely competitive even while having *fun*. They played to win, and I was a lousy player and a happy loser. While fielding, I always tried to grab the right field position because very few balls came that way, and I could stand there and contemplate how I could possibly continue working with them since I disliked them so much. I suppose there is nothing like a friendly fun game to make you realize you really shouldn't be working with these assholes and bitches.

I am laughing as I write this. The woman I am today would have told them exactly where they got off, but back then my only revolt was to refuse to play the next season. They couldn't believe it when I refused, and I was too polite to remind them about how badly they behaved when they lost. They needed me to make up the numbers, and I took unholy delight in refusing to rise to the bait.

Obviously, this wasn't one of the memories I left behind in the wastepaper basket, so it must have been significant, huh?

Now, what is this about having written a letter to me as a teenager with a poem by Pushkin? Looks like your memory is the same as mine since you don't remember what you wrote. Teenagers are roiling, writhing organisms and their emotions run the entire gamut of human feelings before you've even had breakfast. Can you imagine how the rest of their day will be? And that is as it should be. They have this glorious life rolling out before them. To them, love is an entire new world of possibilities.

I remember as a teenager, (yes, this I do remember!) sitting back-to-back on the terrace ledge with a boyfriend and we would read to each other. Two copies of the same book. It was as if we passed on the baton to each other page by page or chapter by chapter. His words undulating into me, backs pressed against each other, and mine doing the same. We read what our parents called *rubbish* and *trash*, but they never stopped this exercise. And the author we read was – I had to go back and Google this, to be honest – Harold Robbins, author of *Never Love a Stranger*, *A Stone for Danny Fisher* and many other books. Ha, ha! I'll bet you were expecting me to mention one of the Great Masters! Believe me when I tell you that there was, at that age, nothing more romantic than the low charged voices of two teenagers dripping with emotion, longing, and yes, possibilities. That, to me, is teenage love. Which never lasted in my case because who wants a boyfriend your parents approve of!

Moving on to your life, as a film maker, I am very interested in hearing about the acrimonious divorce battle. Was your son old enough to intercede on your behalf? How so? Doesn't that make him a confidant in an adult battle where he had to take sides? I'm no expert, but I've heard that children are oddly loyal to both parents even in a failing marriage. Where I lived, parents planning to divorce waited till the youngest was eighteen years old and ready to leave home. It was called empty-nest divorce. All very civilized and sanitized.

What does love mean for adults? I will leave you with your confusion because you seem to be... er... confused. I'm going to assume that all the questions at the end of your letter were more of a stream of consciousness, and you will unearth the answers when you are ready for it. Maybe you can discuss it with your wife, since you seem to be discussing everything about me with her? If she thinks you have a love interest, maybe she can help you sort it out. And you can help her sort out hers, too, since you think she is in love with someone else.

Okay, I was being facetious. Before I descend into sarcasm, I will stop.

Take care,
Tara

PS: I do like this, though. *I believe love is not embedded in duty, responsibility, cause and reason. It is a rage of wind that uproots you from the present, makes your past irrelevant to you and obliterates the significance of a future. Love is happy death.*

February 7th, 2022
Kolkata

Dear Tara,

Ashok Babu did remind me of my mother. And, that too
very deeply.

In 2010 and 2011, I had to travel a lot to Dhanbad on
professional work. I would go by Rajdhani Express from
Howrah to Dhanbad - a three and a half hours journey in
the late afternoon and evening.

As soon as the landscape of Kolkata, and its suburbs
would vanish, there would arise landscapes of paddy
fields, jamun trees, mango trees and bamboo forests
electrified in the golden tinge of a setting sun. As
the dusk gave way to night, I would see my mother in a
red sari, from the bamboo forests, peeping at me at my
coupe's tinted windows strangely with a pathos etched on
her face, I have never seen during her lifetime.

I was married for the first time in 1991 to a girl/woman
with whom I was in love since 1985. Both of us did not want
to become parents for the simple reason that we wanted to
enjoy time with each other as well as with others falling
in-and-out of non-committal relationships. Both of us
had a very high libido quotient, and my wife enjoyed the
company of powerful men whereas I enjoyed the company of
intelligent women. Both of us, in due course of time,
ended up our flings after three to four bouts in bed,
and this happened in a never-ending loop. We smoked, we

drank alcohol, and we were high on drugs. I do not know the driving force in the case of my wife, but in my case, this vulgar playfulness of my life happened because I wanted to suppress my vulnerabilities.

In 1994, my wife decided she wanted to have a baby. Our son was born in 1995. He grew up gradually, a bit because of us, but in spite of us. He was very close to my parents. My wife had already lost her parents by then. In 2008, we separated, completely frustrated with a nebulous life, on the terms that my son would be with me, and I would pay her a one-time alimony of rupees twenty-one lacs, which I did. We agreed that this would result in a mutual consent divorce a year later. She migrated to Edinburg with her then boyfriend, who was also a very close friend of mine.

Once she left the country, she threw several obstacles in my way to prevent a mutual consent divorce. She blackmailed me into parting with more of my wealth. I refused.

Meanwhile, I was a single parent with my son in a house full of servants, maids, and drivers for one and a half years, before I fell in love with my present wife. She moved into my house with her daughter on September 10, 2009, twelve days after the death of my mother. Everything seemed to be in chaos. I had entered into a very complex family situation. For the first time, I felt: I have to rise up to the occasion, if not for anybody else, at least for the sake of these two children. The first two years in this rainbow family were on rocks; about that, I will tell you sometime later.

Surprisingly, my son did not have any relationship with his mother until 2014, after which he and his mother built up a normal relationship, which continues till today. When all my pleadings, requests, and prayers had failed with my wife, my son intervened with his mother saying that if she wanted a normal relationship with him, she would have to agree to a mutual consent divorce with his father. My wife agreed, and the divorce went through.

I was going through my journal yesterday. I found one interesting entry against February 7, 2019, which reads as follows:

In 2015, the Communist Manifesto was the #1 bestseller in the UK.

Today, The Telegraph, Kolkata in arrangement with The Times, London and Reuters published very sad news on its page 2 that vandals have left Karl Marx's memorial stone at the Highgate Cemetery Trust, London, damaged beyond repair in a suspected hammer attack on his grave. It is indeed very painful to read news of such an act of horrendous vandalism.

I am not a spokesperson for any of the various brands of political left. I hate the parliamentary leftists unequivocally.

But I am deeply fascinated by Karl Marx's two ground-breaking theories: 1) Alienation theory postulated in The Economic and Philosophic Manuscripts of 1844. 2) Surplus theory (M − C − M − C …) postulated in Das Kapital (1867).

I reminisce today with great fondness when I was editing a journal namely, Mohana, in Bengali, during my university days where I got the chapters postulating the Alienation theory in The Economic and Philosophic Manuscripts of 1844, translated into Bengali from English by my mathematician and poet friend Shamik Ghosh.

A few months later, I received a postcard from the Archive Cell of the National Library requesting us to meet the Chief Archivist as early as possible. We met him the next day and he informed us that National Library would keep and restore three issues of Mohana covering the Alienation Theory, not only because the translation was very good but more so because this was the first Bengali translation of The Economic and Philosophic Manuscripts of 1844, although partly.

Later when I met a German scholar, three years after, at the Calcutta Book Fair, he explained to me what could be lost in translation for having translated from English, which itself was a translation from original German and there are indeed many significant words in theoretical economics expressed in German that have no equal or even equivalent words in English.

My wife told me the other day that my father is typing out his memoirs. His native place was in the Manikganj sub-division in Dacca, Bangladesh. He was born in 1938. His family migrated to India in 1948, and my parental grandfather settled in a place called Nabadwip in the Nadia district in West Bengal. This is the birthplace of Lord Chaitanya, who is famous all over the world as Chaitanya Mahaprabhu.

Chaitanya Mahaprabhu was a 15th century Indian Saint, who is considered to be the combined avatar of Radha and Krishna by his disciples and various scriptures. Chaitanya Mahaprabhu's mode of worshipping Krishna with ecstatic song and dance had a profound effect on Vaishnavism in Bengal. He was also the chief proponent of the Vedantic philosophy of Achintya Bheda Abheda Tattva. Mahaprabhu founded Gaudiya Vaishnavism. He expounded Bhakti yoga and popularized the chanting of the Hare Krishna Mahamantra. He composed the Shikshashtakam (eight devotional prayers).

He is sometimes called Gauranga or Gaura due to his molten gold-like complexion. His birthday is celebrated as Gaura-Purnima. He is also called Nimai because he was born under a Neem tree.

I spied on my father's memoir a few days back, and I discovered that he has a section, titled: *Ideas*, and I photocopied two of his ideas on prostitution and Hinduism. I reproduce them for you because I found them fascinating:

<u>*Prostitution:*</u>

I present two approaches to prostitution by the State in Europe - 1) the Swedish model, and 2) the German model.

The laws on prostitution in Sweden make it illegal to buy sex, but not to sell the use of one's own body for such services. Procuring and operating a brothel remain illegal. The criminalization of the purchase of sex, but not the selling of one's own body for sex, was unique when first enacted in Sweden in 1999, but since then, Norway and Iceland have adopted similar legislation, both in 2009, followed by Canada in 2014, Northern Ireland in 2015, and France in 2016.

The Swedish Government states that the reason behind this legislation is the importance to society of fighting prostitution.

'Prostitution is considered to cause serious harm both to individuals and to society as a whole. Large-scale crime, including human trafficking for sexual purposes, assault, procuring and drug dealing, is also commonly associated with prostitution. (...) The vast majority of

those in prostitution also have very difficult social circumstances.'

The law is in accordance with Sweden's gender equality program. Theoretically, the gender of the seller and buyer are immaterial under the law, that is it is gender-neutral. However, the law is politically constructed, discussed, and enforced in the context of women selling sex to men. The Swedish Government believes that women selling 'sexual services' to men constitutes a form of violence against women which should be eliminated by reducing demand. Demand for women's sexual 'services' is constructed as a form of male dominance over women, and as a practice which maintains patriarchal hegemony. This legal and social approach to prostitution, which has become known as the 'Swedish Model', needs to be understood – at least partly – in the context of radical feminism (a philosophy which focuses on the theory of the patriarchal roots of inequality between men and women), which is very prominent in Sweden.

Today, the law is largely uncontroversial across the whole political spectrum. The view of prostitution as a legacy of a societal order that subordinates women to men being officially accepted. Consequently, it has become a taboo subject to question the legitimacy and effectiveness of the law, and those who have criticized the law have faced considerable opposition. Nevertheless, there is a body of criticism, within and without parliament, but this has had no measurable effect on the official position and party policy.

Prostitution in Germany is legal, as are all aspects of the sex industry, including brothels, advertisements, and job offers through HR companies. Full-service sex work is widespread and regulated by the German government, which levies taxes on it. In 2002, the government changed the law in an effort to improve the legal situation of sex workers.

<u>Hinduism:</u>

Hinduism is not a monolithic religion that is propagated by the BJP-RSS-VHP combine. I believe Hinduism is not a religion at all but an amalgamation of various schools of thought and philosophies. Scholars regard Hinduism as a fusion or synthesis of various Indian cultures and traditions, with diverse roots and no founder.

In the history of Hinduism, the six orthodox schools had emerged sometime between the start of the Common Era and the Gupta Empire, or around the fourth century. Some scholars have questioned whether the classification of orthodox and heterodox schools is sufficient or accurate, given the diversity and evolution of views within each major school of Hindu philosophy, with some sub-schools combining heterodox and orthodox views.

Since medieval times Indian philosophy has been categorized into āstika and nāstika schools of thought. The orthodox schools of Hindu philosophy have been called ṣaḍdarśana ('six systems'). This scheme was created between the 12th and 16th centuries by Vedantins. It was then adopted by the early Western Indologists and pervades modern understandings of Hindu philosophy.

Āstika

There are six āstika (orthodox) schools of thought. Each is called a darśana, and each darśana accepts the Vedas as authoritative and the premise that ātman (soul, eternal self) exists. The āstika schools are:

1. Samkhya, an atheistic and strongly dualist theoretical exposition of consciousness and matter.

2. Yoga, a school emphasizing meditation, contemplation and liberation.

3. Nyāya or logic, which explores sources of knowledge – Nyāya Sūtras.

4. Vaiśeṣika, an empiricist school of atomism.

5. Mīmāṃsā, an anti-ascetic and anti-mysticism school of orthopraxy.

6. Vedānta, the last segment of knowledge in the Vedas, or jñānakāṇḍa. Vedānta came to be the dominant current of Hinduism in the post-medieval period.

Nāstika

Schools that do not accept the authority of the Vedas are nāstika philosophies, of which four nāstika (heterodox) schools are prominent:

1. Cārvāka, a materialism school that accepted the existence of free will.

2. Ājīvika, a materialism school that denied the existence of free will.

3. Buddhism, a philosophy that denies existence of ātman (soul, self) and is based on the teachings and enlightenment of Gautama Buddha.

4. Jainism, a philosophy that accepts the existence of the ātman (soul, self), and is based on the teachings and enlightenment of twenty-four teachers known as Tirthankaras, with Rishabha as the first and Mahavira as the twenty-fourth.

Other schools

Besides the major orthodox and non-orthodox schools, there have existed syncretic sub-schools that have combined ideas and introduced new ones of their own. The medieval scholar Madhva Acharya (CE 1238–1317) includes the following, along with Buddhism and Jainism, as sub-schools of Hindu philosophy:

1. *Pashupata Shaivism, developed by Nakulisa*

2. *Shaiva Siddhanta, the theistic Sankhya school*

3. *Pratyabhijña, the recognitive school of Kashmir Shaivism*

4. *Raseśvara, a Shaiva school that advocated the use of mercury to reach immortality*

5. *The Ramanuja school*

6. *The Pūrṇaprājña (Madhvācārya) school*

7. *The Pāṇinīya*

The above sub-schools introduced their own ideas while adopting concepts from orthodox schools of Hindu philosophy such as realism of the Nyāya, naturalism of Vaiśeṣika, monism and knowledge of Self (Atman) as essential to liberation of Advaita, self-discipline of Yoga, asceticism and elements of theistic ideas. Some sub-schools share Tantric ideas with those found in some Buddhist traditions.

Do these ideas resonate with you at all?

From my journal, I reproduce a tiny story before ending this letter:

Sometime back I knew a character – Nikhil – who was buoyant and cyclically, depressive; was he some kind of a bipolar.

He was maniacal (although outwardly he lived a normal bachelor life of a public high school teacher) – hypochondriac and sexual – tall, dark, and queerly handsome with sharp dark eyes and long hair.

He would exaggerate his slightest ailments and invent illnesses trapped inside him – liver, pancreas, spleen and kidneys – and go to great lengths to describe them to his coterie; I was one of many.

He hunted for women most unconventionally – doggedly chasing and seducing them with his good looks and strange narratives – and in this matter, he never left anything to chance.

Reportedly, he had great sexual skills and great energy for sex; he was intensely aroused by the sighting of eunuchs…

His anchor was his old ailing father; he took care of his father like a true son.

The guy was finished the day his father died.

And, one day all of a sudden having secured a majestic lock for his ancestral house, he vanished – never to return to the city again.

Surprisingly, nobody talked about him; his collective memory waned over the years.

I felt a strange loneliness without him in the winter evenings for I truly missed his stories of unheard of illnesses and various sexual exploits and adventures!

He also exposed my inadequacies of being a son – selfish and self-centred as I am…

The more I think about this person it seems the more I have moved away from the leitmotif - the idea - of this person.

Bye bye,

Love,
Sandy

February 14th, 2022
Pondicherry

Hi Sandy,

We met at the Delhi airport in 2009. That must have been sandwiched between the end of your first marriage and being in a relationship with your current wife. You were straddling two relationships and going through a lot of turmoil. How is it that I don't remember this detail? Did I spend the whole time talking about myself? For some reason, I walked away from that encounter thinking you were one of those corporate types – what we would generally call *suits*, but without the negative connotation.

I think you spoke to me about your corporate job but did not go into details. You didn't want to talk about the daily grind, you said. It is all coming back to me now. The daily grind could be work or home-related. I never thought to ask. Well, everything, I didn't ask then, I'm asking now.

First, let me get the timeline straight. I like to get events running like a movie in my head. Just my film school training, I guess. It took you and your ex-wife six years to commit to a marriage. Were you both in non-exclusive relationships during those six years? And you came together to be married after six years because you wanted an exclusive relationship with each other? Or did the bed-hopping continue even after you were married? And after your son was born?

Why so many questions, you may ask. I'm trying to work through this maze of complications. I hate shifting goalposts in the middle of the game, but when she changed her mind and wanted to have a baby, you seem to have been okay with the decision. So, it was a mutual decision, right? I hope things settled down for you after he was born – in getting your vulnerabilities under control, or at least managing them better, so as to enjoy the arrival of your son.

Lovely that he was close to your parents. It must have helped while you and your wife got your shit together. Did you? Get your shit together, I mean. Or did you continue with the lifestyle you described while your parents looked after your son?

Look, I'm not being judgmental. I'm one of those people who has to map out everything in my mind and it has to play reel by reel. And it can't roll out that way unless you introduce some conflict into the situation. Hence my use of the language. It is okay if you don't answer any of my questions. It is acceptable for a storyline to have gaps.

Your son was a teenager when you finally called off the marriage with his mother. He must have known what was happening since the man his mother left the marriage for was your friend. Are you still friends with this man? I ask because, for me, I have to make a clean cut and move on. I don't carry tendrils from the past and plant them in my new life.

I do commend your son for developing and maintaining a cordial relationship with his mother as he grew up. Whatever happens, love, understanding and maturity go both ways, and it doesn't matter who reaches out first. If the adult doesn't *adult*, the child becomes the adult.

How did you meet your current wife? And how old was her daughter when you combined households? How did your son adjust from a house that ran only around him, to a blended household? Chaos for the first two years, you say? Ha, ha, can't wait to hear it.

Talking about shifting goalposts in the middle of the game, I must confess I was one of those. I say *was*, but maybe I should say *am*. I don't know because it hasn't been tested since I returned to India from Canada. Somehow in India, women become invisible after a particular age, and you aren't even in the game to protect the goalposts, let alone shift them.

In each of my relationships – several, but three that mattered – I was the one who wanted permanency. Buying a house together, decorating the nursery, having a baby, and the whole married bliss business. But how does one do it when one travels to remote locations for film shooting, some of them with no indoor plumbing but outdoor plumbing, and others with no plumbing at all. I have seen my friends trying to juggle this, but when both are in the same field, one or the other has to miss a work assignment because of baby emergencies. You can't keep an entire crew waiting. So who stays home to take care of the emergency that day, becomes a toss of the coin. Might as well decide if you want to stay together or not with the toss of a coin.

Two of my lovers walked away without a backward glance. Not for lack of caring. Not for lack of love. Goalpost shifted. I moved it. Our years together didn't matter. They liked what we had built together, in fact, they loved the life we had built, but could not open up the circle and embrace fatherhood. I blamed myself when they left. Blamed this deep yearning in me to complete the family circle with a child. Why did I get into these relationships when they were upfront with me that we were only two in the circle? This age-old misplaced wishful thinking that they could be talked into it.

One had been married earlier and was still paying child support for the children to his ex-wife. Babies grew up to be children and children grew up into teenagers and it got expensive, he said. Didn't want to take on more responsibilities. I never met his children. I would have loved to meet them during the weeks he had custody. But I never did.

The other said he would lose me and everything we had together if a baby came between us. As if being a mother made me any less of a lover. He pleaded with me to give up the idea. Relentlessly. It is so hard, you know, to know to weigh the intense, passionate life we had together with the nebulous promise of a child that I thought would complete me. He cried when he left me as if he were being wrenched away from a life he wanted, and I was denying him that life.

I took it very hard, but instead of plunging down a cliff, I played hard, had several flings, and lived life as if to show myself that his leaving did not matter.

The third decided to stay and try it out. Give it a whirl, if that was what it took to be with me. As if we had ordered a new couch for the house, and if it was not comfortable, we could toss it out. He did stay. For my sake, not his. And for that, I was grateful. I wonder if we could have made a family, the kind of family I dreamed about, but my child did not stay long enough for me to find out.

It was winter and it had been snowing. We had a shoot that day. I dressed warm – one of those puffy coats that made you look like a waddling penguin. Can you believe they made them in maternity styles! I was wearing snug sturdy winter boots – not one of those Jimmy Choo or Blanick pencil thin heels with toe cleavage (have you heard of that term?) that I could carry off in my non-pregnant days. I was walking backwards across a meadow, my boots sinking into soft, fluffy snow – it wasn't anything new – something we all did quite often in my profession – walking backwards, I mean. But my foot sank into a rabbit hole, or maybe a raccoon hole under the powdery snow. I stumbled, twisted my ankle and fell hard, buried half under the snow. I thought nothing of it. This was Canada, after all. I got up, shook my foot vigorously and turned it this way and that, and decided I was fine.

That night, I went into premature labour and the rest, as they say, is history. Suffice it to say that we didn't buy a house together, we didn't furnish the nursery together, we didn't raise a child together. He took it harder than I did – if that were possible. And blamed me for all his hurt – I had shifted the goalposts, after all. And given him a glimpse of an *after*. And it had dropped him into this abyss. Never mind that I had fallen into the abyss before him. He blamed me and I blamed my profession. I could have been one of those cubicle dwellers – safe in an overheated office, where there were professional minefields to navigate, not actual burrows and holes that throw your life for a loop.

It didn't hurt to see him go. I didn't want him or any reminders of our life together over the last few months. And he didn't want me, not after what he saw it did to me. I was not the same person. So he moved on.

Dammit, how did I get into this? (Note to self: Avoid minefields in letter writing)

From my abyss,
Tara

PS: There was a lot more in your letter about Karl Marx, religion, Hinduism, hypochondriacs, eunuchs and other unrelated topics. Right now, I am feeling completely shredded and anything I say will come out as the ramblings of a disturbed mind. Maybe, I will respond to those topics in the future, if at all. I would like to hear the story of your father's migration, though.

February 15th, 2022
Kolkata

Dear Tara,

When we met in 2009 at the Delhi Airport, my relationship with my current wife had started for over more than six months. That was the time when I was also struggling to find a publisher for the works that I was writing then.

My ex-wife and I are from the same University. She studied Comparative Literature. I studied Civil Engineering. I would like to believe we were in an exclusive relationship until the time we took the decision of marrying each other. However, today I am not so sure. Looking back, I ask myself: Why I married so early, it seems to be an unending puzzle.

In fact, bed-hopping started from both sides after we were married. It is also because we belonged to a social circle of men and women, who were extremely permissive and were most of the time on alcohol, cigarettes, and drugs. We continued bed-hopping even after our son was born. In retrospect, I believe my ex-wife and I did not know the art of happiness. Somewhere deep within our hearts, we also wanted to mock the institution of marriage. We never got our shit together.

It was only when I took the decision of pursuing the profession of writing seriously in the middle of July 2007, gradually my libido quotient waned. In September 2006, I was detected with Type II Diabetes, but I did not give up on booze, cigarettes, and drugs. I led an erratic and irreverential life of sorts. On April 4, 2008, my ex-wife and I parted ways after she returned from a trip from England, Scotland, and France, which she had taken with her lover and our son. I remember calling my son on hand-phone on March 22, 2008, when he was crossing the English Channel on Eurorail from London to Paris along with his mother and her lover. It was likely that he was aware that his parents were separating. I asked him if he would like to stay with me in Kolkata. He clearly said, he would like to stay wherever his paternal grandparents lived. It was fine with me because they lived in Kolkata, too, although we lived separately.

My son is very sensitive and strong in character. Somehow he took to the significant transition in his life very positively, now that the chaos in the house was completely absent. I had cut down on my booze, cigarettes, and drugs and gave quality time to my son, who in 2008 was only thirteen years old. He improved in his studies, his favourite games of playing chess, swimming, and badminton.

A few months later, I met my current wife through a common friend and fell in love with her at first sight. She was married with a daughter, and her daughter was only six months younger than my son. You would be surprised to know that my current wife and my ex-wife are from the same batch of Comparative Literature Studies at Jadavpur University, both for undergraduate and post-graduate courses. In fact, my current wife had also attended my wedding reception with my ex-wife. I can only conclude and wonder how small the world is! She and I had a whirlwind courtship, and our sexual appetite was similar in nature because of which the relationship was like a bee being attached to a beehive.

The problem was my son fell in love with her daughter, which I came to know many months after we started living together, from September 10, 2009. It was a live-in relationship to start with and the children were of different parents. In the initial years, I was deeply protective of my son, and my current wife [her name, by the way, is Niharika] was deeply protective of her daughter, and in the subterranean, an adolescence love was blooming between my son and her daughter. After almost two years, this went public within the family, and there was very deep acrimony between me and my current wife on account of this. My son suffered from a deep bout of depression, and my daughter was very, very confused. At the end of 2011, I was detected with uncontrolled hypertension and clinical depression and I quit booze, cigarettes, and drugs altogether because my doctor had given up on me.

Meanwhile, in 2010, my first book, *Pentacles* was published followed by *Frosted Glass* in 2011. I continued working on my political crime thriller *Abyss*, even through my dark days.

Happiness has always eluded me. It is further complicated because I am a hyper-rational person, and do not believe in god, and do not give in to any hocus-pocus around spirituality. How I became an atheist is a funny story! When I was a toddler and committed pranks and disobeyed my elders, my elders would curse me that my chest would explode into million pieces, and I would bleed from my wounds for disobeying superior powers. After hours of trepidation and agony, I experienced nothing of such sort happening to me, much to my relief. So, one day I rationalized that there must not be any god if nothing had happened to me in spite of the incriminating curses of my elders.

I started keeping diaries and journaling since the age of fourteen. It was a ritual with me. I wrote about everyday events; what happened at school; the films I watched; the books I read; the delicacies that I ate; the cricket matches that I played; conversations with my parents, school teachers, and friends; the places that I travelled with my parents; my moments of sadness, boredom, and elation, and so many other things. These diaries and journals, written in a stream of consciousness, inflated like novels over the years. My first published book was an anthology of twenty English poems, titled: *Pain*. It was published in 1986 with a gift of rupees two hundred from my mother. It sold in Jadavpur University, Presidency College, and St. Xavier's College in Calcutta like hot cakes.

After I joined the Corporate sector, I wrote on and off in Bengali and English and published some of my poems in renowned literary journals in Calcutta. In 1994, I wrote a play in Bengali, titled: *Ajante*, which was later published in the annual journal of *Bohurupee* in 2010. Between 2002 and 2005, I became an oral storyteller among my friends, colleagues, and relatives - a habit which I started with a lot of passion but gradually waned with time. In 2007, I started writing seriously for pursuing my second profession apart from being a senior engineering professional. And as I mentioned earlier, my first book *Pentacles* was published in 2010. After that, I continued producing book after book, both in the literary format as well as in the technological format.

The other day, I was strolling in a garden in New Town, which is a satellite city of Kolkata, and where I live. I remembered, like a strike of lightning, the poem that I had reproduced in my love letter to you in school. I wonder why, except for the fact that it is a very lovely poem.

That was: *A Winter Evening*, by Alexander Pushkin. It goes as follows:

Sable clouds by tempest driven,
Snowflakes whirling in the gales,
Hark—it sounds like grim wolves howling,
Hark—now like a child it wails!
Creeping through the rustling straw thatch,
Rattling on the mortared walls,
Like some weary wanderer knocking—
On the lowly pane it falls.

Fearsome darkness fills the kitchen,
Drear and lonely our retreat,
Speak a word and break the silence,
Dearest little Mother, sweet!
Has the moaning of the tempest
Closed thine eyelids wearily?
Has the spinning wheel's soft whirring
Hummed a cradle song to thee?

Sweetheart of my youthful Springtime,
Thou true-souled companion dear—
Let us drink! Away with sadness!
Wine will fill our hearts with cheer.
Sing the song how free and careless
Birds live in a distant land—
Sing the song of maids at morning
Meeting by the brook's clear strand!

Sable clouds by tempest driven,
Snowflakes whirling in the gales,
Hark—it sounds like grim wolves howling,
Hark—now like a child it wails!

Sweetheart of my youthful Springtime,
Thou true-souled companion dear,
Let us drink! Away with sadness!
Wine will fill our hearts with cheer!

Bye bye,

Love,
Sandy

February 20th, 2022
Pondicherry

Hi Sandy,

After reading your letter, I was transported back to my film history undergrad classes. To the early days in motion pictures – to the days of film strips… when scenes were cut and spliced, and the film editor left strips of film discarded on the floor.

I have unspooled, unreeled, cut, spliced, reassembled – though patchy – the movie reels of your life in my mind. And that is quite a life! It always takes someone else's experiences to reel in one's perspective of one's own life. Mine feels tame in comparison!

Now I remember – you did mention your search for a publisher when we met at the airport. Looks like your writing has taken off and that struggle is behind you.

It is strange, isn't it, that as adults we look back and scratch our heads over decisions we made when we were younger – all long-term commitments that we had no business getting into. Could hardly take care of ourselves and decided to bring another person into our lives. But my attitude now is – no animals were harmed in the making of this relationship – so we actually made our way out of it with our psyche intact.

Here's a thought – what if you had seen your current wife at your own wedding reception with your first wife, and fallen in love with her at first sight then, instead of eighteen years later? Could have saved so much time and heartbreak. Trivia question: if that had happened, would the Sandy of that time have the gumption to walk out of his own wedding reception and waltz into the sunset with Niharika? My answer to that would be *yes*. What about yours? Maybe gumption is not the right word. How about idealism?

I thought you changed your lifestyle when your son was born, but it looks like it was your writing that lifted you out of rock bottom. We all have our saviours, no matter how they reveal themselves to us.

In my case, I developed an intense antipathy towards my chosen field of work. Talk about spending years of your life getting trained, sharpening your tools, honing your skills, getting name recognition, and then flinging it all over your shoulder and walking away as if none of that mattered. But I lie. Before flinging it away, I spent years wallowing in the depths of misery until my last gasp. And then I emerged, struggling for breath, determined to claw myself out of the abyss and give thanks for the life I had been granted. How dare I disrespect a life that could not make it alive out of my womb by trying to burrow my own life back into the land of the unliving. It took me another few years, but I made it out. Alive.

Where is this permissive community of yours these days? How did you even come across them? College? Work? Social gathering? Soft drugs were quite common when we were growing up. Weed or pot – or ganja as it was called back then. Or Mary Jane (for marijuana) as it was called in Canada. I've been around people doing shrooms. Seen some bad, bad tripping, too. Enough to scare me and keep me away. I guess all of us build our own defence mechanisms around our force fields.

It doesn't sound to me like you were both making a mockery of marriage, because you did get married a second time. After a horrendous first attempt. I always say that the best compliment you can give to the institution of marriage is to go from marriage to marriage. It shows that the institution is strong and has held!

After this, my movie reel gets all tangled and needs careful unravelling. Your son and your stepdaughter fell in love? One hears of these things, but I confess – this is the first time I've heard it first-hand. Oh, the complications! Here you are in a new relationship after years of a marriage from hell and turning your life around, and right in your backyard, the fresh green shoot of a new young romance is blooming. To be perfectly analytical about it, they are not related to each other. They just happen to be related because their parents married each other. But I speak as an outsider. And I have no right to speak of it, because I am not in that living space, going through what you and Niharika had to go through. But to untangle my movie reel, am I allowed to ask if it all got resolved, after the bout of depression? Must have, right? Because you are still married. And you still continue to live in Calcutta instead of fleeing to a distant island.

For me, I was really torn. If I left Canada, was I abandoning the memories of my life there? Rejecting everything that happened there? I tried a couple of times to come back to India. Strange – because I never thought of it as home, but as a destination to escape to. Maybe I didn't escape to the right city – I fled right back after a year or two. Maybe I picked the wrong city. Tried Delhi the first time. What a superficial and farcical city! Tried Bangalore the next time. Even today when this city tops the *best of* in several categories, I roll my eyes and wonder how they came up with that. You were right in your ballad when you spoke of *heat, dust, and humidity of our places, and the festering wounds of impoverishment everywhere.* I ran back to Canada again. But *third time's a charm,* as they say. Someone told me about Pondicherry, and I arrived there determined to make it work. I didn't have to try very hard. It appealed to me. Several years later, I'm still here. Someday I will share anecdotes of my attempted attempts at *ghar wapsi,* though it was several years before I got really and truly *wapsi*-ed! Many years were spent getting ghar un-*wapsi*-ed.

You can write in Bengali! Aren't you blessed! I feel so inadequate that I can't write in any other language except English. The drawback of a colonial upbringing.

Thanks for the poem you were meant to give me way back in school. Are you sure it wasn't because your feelings were like *Snowflakes whirling in the flakes?* I was going to mention *Speak a word and break the silence* but it is followed by *Dearest Little Mother, sweet!* which I don't think is for me. But yes, it is a lovely poem written by Pushkin while he was isolated under house arrest. And I am glad you waited so many years to share it with me when I am at a stage where I can appreciate the poem.

During my years in Canada, I began a love affair with political poetry. It happened when I wandered into a poetry slam one day and got exposed to spoken word poetry performances. From there into the world of political poems. After that, I became a groupie. I learned so much about the country I lived in by foraging and deep-diving into the poetry slam world. Things I had known only via prose which were now being performed from the heart right before me, and it reached in and wrenched my feelings out of me. It was also during the days when a president across the border decided to play hopscotch in countries with his military might, while all the time assuring the people in those countries that he was *liberating* them. War on Terror. Shock and Awe. Opposition to his war mongering spewed out in these poetry sessions. And I was captivated. To see and hear my feelings performed on a stage before me!

I'll go through my collection and see if I can locate a couple of them for you.

Until then, take care,
Tara

February 21st, 2022
Kolkata

Dear Tara,

I think my lifestyle changed after I started writing seriously in 2007. And the next year, came the sole responsibility of my son in 2008!

The permissive community that I talked of came from my days at the Jadavpur University. Well, I was into all sorts of things: weed, ganja, marijuana, charas, and later heroin, as well. Coming out of it was harrowing, considering that I already had uncontrolled hypertension and clinical depression.

I think my children understood after the first two years where they belonged, and in spite of the depression, heartburn and heartaches, if not like brothers and sisters, they started behaving with each other like friends. That was comforting to me and Niharika and slowly eased our life.

This was the time when I wrote a simple poem about my children, which reads as follows:

My children

Sometimes I love you like my own sister
Sometimes I love you like my dearest friend
Sometimes I love you like my beloved

Oh stepsister! I do not know the boundaries of my love

Sometimes I love you like my own brother
Sometimes I love you like my dearest friend
Sometimes I love you like my beloved

Oh stepbrother! I do not know the boundaries of my love, too

Oh stepsister! I hate you too when you avoid me and gang up with your university friends

Oh stepbrother! As if I do not hate you so strongly when you do the same

My children, love has no boundaries, after all
My children, love is mysterious and yet to be understood in spite of all the human inventions

Sometimes I am fearful of the futures of both of you – the separate ways you will have to traverse finally in your not-so-distant lives

I told you the stories of my children – my anxieties and my fears

You comforted me by saying:
Children will be children, and,
Love will be love, be that of any kind
Instead, you told me the story of a man who to beat his agonies of the uncertainties of his life
Amassed enormous wealth and real estate and ornaments
Yet he could not get over his agonies, rather became a depressed wreck in the long run

In the end, you said: Sandy dear, take some rest and let some things take shape as they are destined to be

Cheating and betrayal are in my blood. I have betrayed Niharika as well, and in 2014, I was caught red-handed by Niharika sex-texting one of my girlfriends while Niharika was busy with the admissions of my son and daughter to colleges. I betrayed Niharika to a point when she was so hurt that I understood the consequences of my actions. Somehow it healed me from inside. Although, it changed the equation between me and Niharika for the years to come. Well, Niharika was at the wedding reception of my first wife. I did not fall in love with her at that time. The love at first sight happened much later.

Both my wives have told me, including my other girlfriends, that I am not a one-woman-man, and I am not the marriageable kind. Yet I have married two times. Let me tell you, I believe marriage is the worst institution man has created on this planet for the purposes of straightening out inheritance protocol in a patriarchal society. Period.

I came across a jotting in my journal the other day:

In my earlier life, I was a camel. In my next life, I want to be an elephant and thereafter, I want to be a giant tree fern in an African rainforest.

In 1988, at *Nandan*, I happened to watch *The Sacrifice* at a film festival, and the film had a deep impact on me. I have not watched the film again, but its plot and visuals are etched on my soul like the magical and intense impact that *Aparajito* and *Pratidwandi* (both the films I have watched more than 15 times) have had on me.

The Sacrifice (1986), director Andrei Tarkovsky's final film, begins in Bergmanesque fashion on a small, remote island, where friends and family gather for drama critic Alexander's (Erland Josephson) birthday celebration. The revelry is interrupted by a radio announcement: World War III has begun, and Mankind is only hours away from utter annihilation. Each of the guests reacts differently to the news: the most dramatic response is Alexander's, who promises God that he'll give up everything he holds dear--including his beloved 6-year-old son — if war is averted. Allan Edwall, a local mailman with purported mystical powers, offers to intervene with the Creator on Josephson's behalf. The Sacrifice is acutely dependent upon its visuals and overall mood. The willingness of Tarkovsky's protagonist to forego all his possessions may well have sprung from the cancer-ridden director's awareness that he, too, would soon be giving up everything to face his Maker (Tarkovsky was a deeply religious man). *The Sacrifice* won four awards at the Cannes Film Festival, including the Grand Prix.

The first film that I watched without telling my parents was in the autumn of 1977, a Hindi potboiler musical – *Hum Kisi Se Kum Naheen*. I was then in Class VII and watched the film in Preet Palace, Ludhiana. I told my parents that I was going to play a cricket match. I had gone for the 4 pm show and by the time I returned home it was already 7.15 pm and my father was back from the office. I hurriedly pedalled my bicycle on my way back home all the time tremulous about being caught the moment I reached. Over dinner, my father enquired about my performance in the afternoon cricket match. I was absentmindedly crooning, *Bachna Hain Hasinoon*. Reacting like a sniper, I replied reflexively that I had taken 3 wickets including one of the opening pair batsmen and scored a vital quarter-century to win the match.

Having gained the mental strength with one film, I consolidated my strength by watching more and more films afternoon after afternoon stealthily by neglecting my games and studies because by that time I got addicted to the silence and darkness of cinema halls.

Even now I run away from family and work to watch films alone although I would say in the long run of the intervening forty-one years I have been able to improve my taste in films.

The pandemic has changed this habit of mine.

We all originate out of the ancient, primitive wilderness. Man by virtue of his intelligent consciousness created civilization by manipulating, and destroying nature, and its other living constituents, and finally bred domesticity to his life. Domesticity further bred a kind of strange loneliness, which created a need for alternative companionship. Instead of running back to the wilderness for seeking unfettered freedom (like Michael K in the Life and Times of Michael K by J M Coetzee) among nature comprising animals in their natural habitat, and wild flora and fauna, and feeding himself with his own produce, he started domesticating timid animals and bringing flora and fauna to his own home in the form of gardens and pets, respectively. Adopting nature is almost adopting death. It requires an earnestness, which one finds in the fictional character of Michael K and not in oneself. Whereas domesticating nature is adopting 'love for animals and nature.' After I read Michael K, I could not read any book or watch any movie for more than two months; it had such a telling impact on me. Yes, you have guessed it right – I am not in favour of keeping pets or growing gardens at home. My father's house has aesthetically grown gardens in the front and back yard, car track and on the terrace, thanks to my mother's groundwork and the hardworking gardeners working in the house. We have never had pets since our childhood. I must confess: I have a strange love for aquariums. We had a large aquarium in our house when I was a child.

Like how greedy or lusty can a person get? How deep can somebody excavate an abyss within the bowels of this earth and live inside it happily drowned in vain glory? How dark should an abyss get filled with its endless operations of greed and lust before its occupants or its chief architect run for some sunshine for a change?

Bye bye,

Love,
Sandy

February 25th, 2022
Pondicherry

Oh Sandy, your poem *My Children* tugged at my heart strings. It must have been so hard for them – being that young, in a situation not of their making, and not knowing the boundaries of love. I went back to your first letter and feel happy to hear that they have both moved on and are doing well in their lives.

Wasn't there a movie about ten years ago about a 118-year-old man, the last mortal on earth, with a similar story? *Mr Nobody*, if my memory is right.

Jesus, Sandy, do you have to throw a bombshell in every letter! This one is *my children are okay now, but I'm a serial cheater*. Do you remember the joke that went around when we were young? At least it was a joke in Ludhiana where earthy jokes are taken in stride. Don't know how the rest of the country would have taken it. A guy says he does not smoke, drink alcohol or eat non-veg except on occasion. What occasion? He smokes only when he is drinking alcohol. When does he drink alcohol? Only when he eats non-veg. When does he eat non-veg? Only when he is out whoring. When is he out whoring? Er… every day??

Bad joke? Just one more thing before I go back to behaving my age… I have never understood why we paint smoking, drinking alcohol, and eating non-veg with the same tar brush? In my world, being corrupt, indifferent to the suffering of others, cruelty to animals, inciting hate and violence, and so many other inhumane things should receive the tar brush first.

I should have added a swipe of the tar brush over vegetarian evangelists, but it is not my intention to use our letters to get on my soap box. Maybe I should unleash my carnivore Canadian friend on them who said – *Of course, I'm a vegetarian. I eat vegetables, don't I?*

Back to your bombshell… Why do you say cheating and betrayal are *in your blood*? Do these characteristics run across generations? All that betrayal and hurt that follows – how do you mend a relationship after that? It is like saying I've quit smoking and having people sniff discreetly around you. Not being a one-woman man is your business, but doesn't juggling more than one relationship at a time get stressful and energy draining? All that subterfuge, trying to keep your lies straight, remembering what you said where…

I've always found it easier to close out one relationship before moving on to the next. That way there is no danger of calling out the wrong name in the throes of passion if you know what I mean. But then, I never did get married, so I can't vouch for marriage being the worst man-made institution. You say it is because of inheritance in a patriarchal society. I always thought of it as the need for sanctioned sex within the boundaries of a contract; which is why it makes no sense these days. But getting married does seem to be a popular pastime!

Preet Palace! Et tu, Sandy? How come we never ran into each other? I've lost count of how many times I snuck away there to watch movies. It was like the forbidden fruit. There was a daredevil feeling that you were living life to the full when you snuck in there in bright daylight for the 4 pm show and emerged three hours later to a sky almost as dark as the theatre you crept out from. Your ears still ringing with the song-and-dance sequences of gyrating bodies and coquettish come-hither looks.

You probably left Ludhiana after high school, but I did a year of college there before I left for Canada. It could be loosely termed as *a year of college*. More time was spent in the movie theatres. No one at home knew of my antics. I left home at the regular time and returned home when I was expected back. If I was late, there was always the quintessential *special class* that is like getting an unlimited free pass from Indian parents. They were *special classes* - in what was something I hid from my parents!

One movie that really deceived me in its perspective was *Gone with the wind* starring Clark Gable and Vivien Leigh. Can't remember if Preet Palace ran it. However, as a teenager and even beyond, I saw it whenever it came as a rerun. Drooled over Clark Gable. Believed every scene of its portrayal. Grieved over *Frankly my dear, I don't give a damn.*

It took one movie discussion session later in Canada to see it through a racial lens. Here I was gushing over it, and there was a woman of colour across the room giving me the stink-eye, except that I took it for an admiring gaze! Everyone else started shifting uncomfortably in their chair and gazing at a point on the wall just over my right shoulder. Coming from India where people don't make eye contact, I thought nothing of it. After I was done, that woman very gently and politely tore my analysis to pieces, but it felt like I (or rather, my ignorance) was peeled away layer by layer. Only then did I understand the racial insensitivity, the slurs, the glorification of the Ku Klux Klan, and the rose hued portrayal of the South. In the scene where Rhett Butler leaves Scarlett and goes to join the Confederate Army – that scene where we cried because he was abandoning her – we should have been questioning which army he was going to join.

I hauled my sorry ass home, feeling decimated, unsure of myself and woefully aware of my ignorance. But that did not stop me from going for the next discussion. I think she liked it that I came back for other discussions and that I didn't get defensive. We became friends – her name was Betsy – and she taught me so much in the years that we've known each other. I liked her because she opened my eyes to the world around me, and taught me to question, interrogate and think for myself.

And now if you remember – can you let me know if Preet Palace ran English movies? Or am I thinking about some other movie theatre?

The pandemic has made me turn to OTT platforms to catch up on movies and serials, but there is nothing like burrowing into the dark cave of movie theatres, wrapping yourself with the sound effects, suspending belief and letting the movie permeate through your pores. And after it is over, surfacing dazed and blinking into the real world. No matter how much we try to replicate that effect at home by investing in more and more sophisticated home theatres, there is something lost by moving away from going to movie theatres.

Also, the mushrooming of OTT platforms has muddied the waters between good, mediocre, and positively horrendous movie making. Add serials to the list, too.

This garden you speak of – in your father's house – is this where you live now? And you don't mind it as long as there are people to tend to it? I don't have a garden and pets for one reason – I like to keep myself nimble to leave whenever I want to without worrying about the length of my absence. Don't need to find a pet sitter. No need to come back to plants you've killed through sheer neglect.

When I do feel the need for gardens, I wander into the Pondicherry Botanical Gardens and spend some time there. Close enough to the centre of town, so one doesn't have to travel too far out or make elaborate plans in advance. It was created in 1826 and has a very French influence. Not very big – a little over 20 acres or so, but it does have an aquarium which may be of interest to you! I, too, find aquariums calming.

Your last para was quite concerning, and I'm not sure what brought that on. Throwing a little light over the words may help…

In my last letter, I mentioned sharing a couple of poems with you from the poetry slam. I couldn't find the one I wanted, but while foraging among my boxes, I found one about cricket that really spoke to me when I was at that performance. This was back in the MySpace days when artists used to come for performances with their poetry printed in little booklets and CDs of their work which you could buy for a combination rate of ten dollars or so.

The booklet has a statement by the great cricket writer, historian and statesman C.L.R. James.

"An artistic, social event does not reflect the age. It is the age. Cricket I want to say most clearly, is not an addition or a decoration or some specific unit that one adds to what really constitutes the history of a period.

Cricket is as much part of history as books written are a part of history."

The artist, who was from Trinidad, performed two poems. You could close your eyes and be transported to the cricket field during his performance. One, about Vivian Richards, was titled 'Dragon Slayer'. Here are a few random stanzas from that performance:

…

…

swaggered across the grounds
to what might be a slow hand
clap if he was at home   or a hush
if he was to explode
on a foreign theatre

arms windmilling slowly as he came
in his desire to dominate overwhelming

Viv taught us how to walk
shoulders thrown back and always
smiling like he knew the secret
meaning of a song everyone
was humming

…

…

Viv knew how to look good
returning to the pavilion
when he had made 291 at Lord's
or a duck   the ultimate knightly code

how to carve dignity
out of nothing
of which we sometimes
believed we were made

Unfortunately, I cannot share the name of the artist - a few years later I was trying to locate him to buy a few copies of his booklets and found that there were allegations of sexual harassment against him. Again, the dilemma of separating the art from the artist. Another one bites the dust...

Take care,
Tara

March 1st, 2022
Kolkata

Dear Tara,

I want to address your point in the last letter: Are cheating and betrayal in our genes? I think it is the way devotion and fidelity are. The conflict between these two extremes takes place in our nervous system forever. Some people are better at controlling the push and pull of cheating and betrayal in their genes. Some are not, like me. Generally, I believe my conscience pricks less than it should. Although, one of the neuro-psychiatrists that I visited told me, that I do have a strong conscience. But I believe, I do not have a strong conscience. Otherwise, I would not have cheated on my wives and lovers so rampantly. At the same time, I must tell you, I have always felt guilty about my aberrant acts. I have caused hurt to a lot of people. Sometimes I have cared. Sometimes I have not cared. Today these memories affect me deeply.

I would like to share with you two journal entries on the subject of marriage that you might find bizarre.

1. *My problem with the idea of marriage is: Cohabitation till death do us apart. Companionship is a fantastic idea. But it does not require two persons to stay together forever. They can also intermittently stay together and stay apart depending upon their mutual interests and choices. The psychosomatic zing and razzmatazz between two individuals in love*

are converted to habitual affection in marriage and replaces passion with compassion, and further transports a private matter into the domain and control of the State. Marriage in many instances limits the pursuits and aspirations of individuals in other fields. It robs you of your individuality.

My idea is: An individual should be firmly rooted in his adjoining community, which in turn should be a conglomeration of individuals who have migrated to a place out of various necessities or have been staying together for ages. Individuals will eventually fall in love (most of the time with multiple persons) and explore sexual choices and will also reproduce in some cases. The community as a whole in a comprehensive manner will have to take care of its individuals through collaboration and not competition.

The idea of conquest is a futile idea in the world of love. It should be destroyed forever in the dust of community existence.

2. *In The Outsider, Meursault does not cry at his mother's death. This post-WWII path-breaking novella is a milestone in 20ᵗʰ century literature and unravels many deeper secrets of modernity, and post-modernity, which would be realized by humanity much later: the modern era has systemically destroyed and deconstructed the intensity of human emotions. The tragic romantic fables of Shirin-Farhad; Laila-Majnu, and Romeo-Juliet now seemed like relics of the past. Yet, Orhan Pamuk could narrate the intense romantic tale (yes, again a tragedy) of Kemal Bey and Fuzun in the environs of modern Istanbul believably in The Museum of Innocence. That is the*

magic of Pamuk's writing. I have read this modern epic twice and visited the Museum (built to Pamuk's vision) at Nisantasi in Istanbul with Niharika, and my children. When you read about, and watch the 1473 cigarette butts smoked by Fuzun in Kemal Bey's personal collection you are in awe of Kemal Bey's paranoid love for Fuzun, his cousin, apart from being amazed at the evolution of the cigarette industry in modern Istanbul. I believe, in the literature of the last 100 years, if The Outsider is one end of a swinging pendulum, then The Museum of Innocence is another end.

I have always believed intense monogamist love requires a unique kind of capability, and genetic arrangement, which very few individuals possess at any point in time.

Yet, I have often wondered whether it is possible for an evolved human being to be involved in intense multiple amorous relationships at the same time (can Romeo have many Juliets or Juliet have many Romeos?). Having multiple sex partners is one thing (our secret wish for such a phenomenon is very realistic as we are all polygamous/polyandrous individuals – I refer to Shakespeare's Midsummer Night's Dream and anthropologist Desmond Morris); but I am talking about something quite different. Having examined the issue from various angles I have arrived at the conclusion: It is not possible (because of pinpricks of guilt, time management, and logistics). Yet, a modern man/woman can be seen experiencing multiple relationships concurrently. Modernity is all about greed-guzzling, and this has infused in the modern individual a unique greed for sexual conquest in the name of relationship-building. This is distinctly *different from keeping a harem. The modern man is besotted with sexual adventurism, yet he won't take recourse to an elite whorehouse, but rather chase a woman secretively in the name of love to take her to bed as fast as possible in the end.*

I am planning to explore a story: A man is in an intense relationship with a woman, yet the circumstances of his life are such that to avoid falling into a mental trap and distract from his boredom, losses, unhappiness, and failures of his life, starts spending some time in an elite whorehouse, and gets addicted to this habit. He goes through a vortex of turbulent emotions. The story would be a study of these turbulent emotions.

Gone with the wind is a racist film. Because I had watched this film at the age of twenty when my political views were formed I could see beneath the layers.

Vivian Richards is a very favourite cricketer of mine almost in the same vein as Sunil Manohar Gavaskar is. I have listened to and watched their games - worst and best - when I was growing up. But one must remember while evaluating these two greats that Vivian Richards did not have to play the fiery pace battery of his own team in international matches whereas Sunil Manohar Gavaskar had to. I love Vivian Richards because of his charisma and the machismo he built around himself. He used to be cool, sexy, and breezy. Almost the way I loved Mats Wilander, the Swedish former world number one tennis player, and George Best, the Northern Irish footballer, who never got a chance to play in a World Cup match.

I have always held the opinion that even sexual offenders need to be given a chance to be heard. I strongly believe they can even be rehabilitated and brought into the mainstream. Some of the sexual offenders have been very creative people like Woody Allen, Roman Polanski, and Kevin Spacey. A civilization is judged by the way you treat its aberrant citizens. I think because of the general increase in the level of information across the world we are getting to know about sexual offenders more and more in our societies. It is significantly important to understand their minds and know why they do what they do so that such behaviour can be treated in future.

In my childhood, I had a beautiful and romantic and platonic relationship with my maternal first cousin, who was two years junior to me. We had a lovely melodious universe of ours, which our family members misunderstood. Today, she is married to the love of her adolescent years and is a mother of two grown-up children. I feel very awkward facing her when we run into each other. I do not know, why?

I have been involved with ultra-left politics during my university years. Because of my study of various political philosophies, I no longer subscribe to ultra-leftism. However, I cannot shy away from the fact that my heart has always been very close to the political movements on the ground.

In this connection, I will put before you a journal entry that I had written during the time of the Shaheen Bagh protests.

The landscape comprises two extremes: The fire-fly-like shining armour of Shaheen Bhag spread all across India and the farce spread by the toxic duo of President Trump – Prime Minister Modi from Ahmedabad to Agra, is invigorating the rattlesnake trapped inside my soul.

The fear of statelessness is lionizing average Muslim women who were home-bound until now. This is a flash point in history. The opportunism of President Trump is to woo the NRIs in the USA who did not vote for him in the last election in large numbers. By lending political legitimacy to this circus, Prime Minister Modi wants to deflect the growing protestations, throughout India, against the CAA and abrogation of Article 370.

Yesterday's news informs us Delhi is likely to burn in the days to come. Maybe many more cities, towns and villages will follow.

The brilliant thing about the Communists of yesteryears in Bengal was that they were scholarly, read contrary views and questioned even the most transparent of matters. In 1987 during my university days, I was introduced to a Revolutionary Communist who placed before me the relevant Constituent Assembly debates, correspondence between the leaders of that time and the factual history of migration between 1947 and 1948 from West Pakistan to India. He laid before me a dissection of why the Permit Card was not made applicable to migrants of East Pakistan and taught me to sift through this enormous pile of documents, at the end of which I concluded the Indian Citizenship Law by itself is flawed and practised in a biased manner throughout history.

One of the greatest contributions of Indian Communists in polemics was their scholarly critique of the Indian Constitution until the middle of the 1980s and also of the intriguing politics of Mohandas Karamchand Gandhi.

But whatever is left of the Indian Citizenship Law, one can argue and build up a cogent case [on the basis of its remnants] against CAA being unconstitutional as it is incomplete and open to multifarious ambiguities.

When I talked to this Revolutionary Communist yesterday, who is very old and ill now, about the rattlesnake trapped inside my soul, transmitting venom throughout my veins and that I was in a constant fit of rage, he advised me: Do not cool down; this is the time to return in waves; jump out of your castle for once!

Regarding my Jadavpur University days, I had a journal entry, which I thought I should share with you that would throw some light on my university.

I did my Civil Engineering from Jadavpur University in 1988. Niharika did her under-graduation and post-graduation in Comparative Literature from Jadavpur University. My daughter, Meghna is studying in the Department of International Relations, Jadavpur University and pursuing her under-graduation in Political Science and presently she is in her second year. The deviant in our family is: my son, who studies at IIEST, Shibpur (a Central Government Institute under the MHRD in the likes of IITs and NITs) and he is presently pursuing his dual (integrated) B.Tech-M.Tech degree in Civil Engineering.

I think JU has had an indelible impact on my view of life, way of life, tastes, ethics, choices, etc. It is an institution with a very rich tradition and a liberal and empathetic vision. JU, I have seen, always has a magical impact on its students. In fact, I am pleasantly surprised by my daughter's transformation into a lady of deep understanding, empathy and maturity after enrolling herself in JU.

JU is also famous for rising to the cause and responding positively to global issues. The present example being the Solidarity Movement with the JNU students.

JU was started as the National Council of Education in 1905 and the foundation of the NCE was made possible by the munificence – scholarly as well as monetary – of the *likes of Raja Subodh Chandra Mallik, Brajendra Kishore Roychowdhury of Gouripur as well as Sir Rash Behari Ghosh (First President of NCE), poet Rabindranath Tagore and Aurobindo Ghosh. After independence, the Government of West Bengal, with the concurrence of the Government of India, enacted the necessary legislation to establish Jadavpur University on the 24th of December 1955.*

During my four-year stint at JU, I had participated in many Solidarity Movements notably against the Arwal massacre in 1986. It was nothing but a high-level conspiracy hatched at the Ministerial and Secretariat level of the then Bihar Congress Government to terrorize and suppress the legal and democratic movement of the poor peasants and agricultural labourers, the movement of casual industrial labourers in the Hindustan Lever factory at Garden Reach, and the movement of the industrial labourers in Standard Batteries factory at Ballygunge. I had also participated in movements that concerned JU and its essence, like the Hostel Movement resulting in the construction of more hostels for students, the Quota Movement resulting in the abolition of the management quota, and the Departmental Movement against cheating and copying, resulting in improved management of internal examinations in the Department of Civil Engineering.

I am not so sure whether students nowadays in JU are concerned about issues pertaining to JU. I do not get to hear much about them. JU when compared to IIEST has a horrendous track record of semester management. In IIEST, the odd semester is of 5 months and the even semester is of 4 months, thereby leaving 3 months for the students to pursue hobbies, passions, foreign language classes and internships/training of various kinds. JU semesters and starting of classes for the next session are back to back. Academic calendars are not published in JU on time. Examination calendars are not given to students on time. Cheating and copying in JU examinations are rampant. Are these not issues to protest and ensure that things are corrected in a manner that would help the students in getting quality education? It is very important to be in solidarity with global issues but it is also very important to raise local issues.

Secondly, I think, the Engineering faculty, the Arts faculty and the Science faculty are increasingly becoming water-tight chambers. In our time, it was not so; two of my best friends are from the Mathematics Department and the English Department. The club activities of JU are also going down. In our time the clubs were very active.

Students of JU, if they want to maintain the tradition of JU, need to concentrate on these issues as well.

I am deeply disturbed by the on-going war Russia has inflicted on Ukraine. My heart is heavy; I would like to end with a poem, titled: Sometimes.

Sometimes

Sometimes, only sometimes - for a fraction of a few seconds
I can feel time passing on the wind blowing carelessly through the flowers of spring
I can feel the diurnal motion of the earth around its axis
I can feel waves rising and forming in the oceans
I can feel mountains climbing a few nanomillimeters into the sky
I can feel millions of clouds getting pregnant with crystals of water

Sometimes, only sometimes – for a fraction of a few seconds
I can feel the velocity of sunlight reaching us at dawn

I can feel molten magma locomoting wildly below the earth's ravaged crust
I can feel myself falling through a black hole endlessly
I can feel the scents of celestial gardens reaching up to my nostrils
I can feel engines pumping into my feet to run through the impenetrable jungles of our land as I could do in my youth
I can feel the deathly darkness of mountain gorges

Sometimes, only sometimes – for a fraction of a few seconds
I can see my reflection on my son's beautiful face

It is in those few moments of acute loneliness that I feel absolutely and irrevocably united with myself

Bye bye,

Love,
Sandy

March 10ᵗʰ, 2022
Kolkata

Dear Tara,

I was the first one, among both of us, to write the first letter to you. Ironically you never asked, why! There must be a reason why I wrote to you after all these years.

Frankly speaking, I am fed up and frustrated with my wasted life. Today, I do not have any friends. There are moments of extreme darkness and loneliness when I feel like crying. But I cannot cry. It is as if my tear glands have gone dry. The moments, when you feel like crying and are not able to cry, are horrendous and unbearable.

I have been a hedonist animal all my life in terms of food, physical comfort, leisure and sex.

In the ballad I had written, I am a bureaucrat. No, I am not a bureaucrat. I am a senior engineering professional, a very passionate engineering professional. My life has followed the speed of a rocket, although I wanted to be a leisurely philosopher.

In my profession as an engineer, I have worked at a breakneck speed. As an author since 2010, I have published eight literary works and three technical works. I have done so many things, have been prolific, achieved a lot; yet, I have never achieved happiness or peace of mind.

I have sought pleasure in the brothels of Zurich, Melbourne, Bangkok, and Sao Paulo in exotic environment, yet, nothing has given me peace.

I do not know, how a man can achieve happiness or peace! Does one have to scream to achieve that?

One night I dreamt of you cycling in slow motion to school, our beloved Sacred Heart Convent School in Ludhiana, in our winter dress; I could almost feel the chill in my sleep. When I woke up, I decided, I have to write to Tara. You seemed like a signal in the darkness.

The first moon-rise that I sighted was in 1999 idling alone on Marina Beach in Madras. Initially what I saw was a growing crimson halo spreading across the horizon followed by a glowing pale reddish ball steadily making its way up in the sky from the bowels of the ocean. Then all of a sudden a mysterious reddish moon was hanging in the sky faintly illuminating the universe with its ethereal haze. That night I dreamt of carrying a moon on my back up an arduous rocky cliff.

How do you feel when you paraglide?

I paraglided in Pokhara in 2006. Paragliding is available in Pokhara for a long time and you will be flying in the Annapurna region, most specifically above the Pokhara Valley and the Fewa Lake. Fewa Lake is just below the Fishtail and Annapurna mountain and the views from above the lake while you paraglide are tremendous. You float over mystery-shrouded monasteries, brilliant turquoise lakes, raging Himalayan rivers, exotic jungles and villages forgotten in time.

For a change, I have sniffed some cocaine tonight. Feeling like as though I am floating in the air, flying to Mount Everest.

I boarded the mountain flight to Mount Everest in the year 2006.

Only awe-filled silence can come close to matching the experience of going on a mountain flight to encounter the tallest mountains on earth. No wonder mountain fly-bys have become a popular tourist attraction in Nepal.

As the plane moves along, the mountains come closer and closer.

Next on the vision is Choba-Bhamare, the smallest one at 5,933m but singularly stubborn as it has never been climbed.

Then appears the mountain that is not only prominent in sight but also spirituality - Gauri-Shanker. Lord Shiva (Shanker) and his consort Gauri are said to protect this mountain, at a proud height of 7,134m. This summit had a history of unsuccessful attempts till 1979. Gauri-Shanker is sharp and very conspicuous during the mountain flight.

As the plane moves towards the land of the rising sun, the eastern Himalaya, a succession of glorious mountains follow. Melungtse, a plateau like mountain, stretches up to 7,023m.

Chugimago at 6,297m is still a virgin, waiting to be climbed.

At 6,956m, Numbur mountain resembles a breast, the maternal source in the sky providing pure milk to the Sherpas of the Solukhumbu.

Next is Karyolung, an intensely white mountain that at 6,511m gleams with the rising sun.

Cho-Oyu is the eighth highest mountain in the world, reaching a height of 8,201m, it appears stunningly beautiful from the aircraft.

Next on the menu is Gyachungkhang, at a majestic height of 7,952m, considered an extremely difficult climb.

To the right of Gyachungkhang is Pumori (7,161m).

As passengers get closer to Everest, there's Nuptse (7,855m), which means West Peak, signifying its direction from Everest.

Finally, there's Everest (8,848 m), known as Sagarmatha by the Nepalese and Chomolungma by the Tibetans. Much has already been written about Everest, but to witness it face to face during a mountain flight is inspiring. Even while it looms in front of the eyes, it remains an enigma, this highest spot on earth.

Images and dreams are coming back to me. I am becoming lighter. I rummage my photo albums and my journals. Will I get some peace when I see the angel-like faces of my children when they were infants? They are grown up and have no time for me now. Niharika does not understand me. We are from different planets. For the last one week, I have been thinking about the question of identity, which I wanted to write about to you in my last letter, but I forgot and then I suddenly came across an excerpt from Milan Kundera's *Identity* quoted in my journal.

'… he has been thinking about it: the eye: the window to the soul; the centre of the face's beauty; the point where a person's identity is concentrated; but at the same time an optical instrument that requires constant washing, wetting, maintenance by a special liquid dosed with salt. So the gaze, the greatest marvel man possesses,

is regularly interrupted by a mechanical washing action. Like a windscreen washed by a wiper. And nowadays you can even set the tempo of the wind-screen wiper in such a way that the movements are separated by a ten-second pause, which is, roughly, an eyelid's rhythm.'

Today, as I stand on the terrace, I can see in the sky, the slow dance of infinite stars and you in your teenage years cycling in slow motion towards a reddish moon in the winter dress of our school. How elegant and appealing you look. My heart is so corroded and abraded with the wasteful experiences of my life that even such a sparkling visualization does not generate calm and poise in my soul.

Tara, what sort of an animal am I?

Bye bye,

Love,
Sandy

March 10th, 2022
Pondicherry

Hi Sandy,

You've done quite a lot of jumping around in your letter. I might have to resort to the same in my reply.

I will start with your comments about sexual offenders. I wonder if women tend to think about it differently. With the names that you mention, as I said earlier, it becomes difficult to separate the art from the artist. In my case, I have stopped watching any movies or shows associated with them. What I'd like to see is accountability and taking personal responsibility for their acts. I find it particularly egregious... no, never mind. This is such a vast subject that we could go on and on over several discussions. Don't forget to add Jeffrey Epstein to the list, though he was not an artist, but a con artist.

Did you notice that your comments about betrayal in a marriage and your journal entries about marriage telescope into each other?

Conscience? Genes? I don't know. Way back one of my male friends told me – people don't cheat if there is a chance they will get caught. So, the only thing that keeps people from straying is the fear of getting caught? Which basically brings a relationship down to a policing activity. Somewhat like a parent doing a sniff-test around a teenager for traces of smoking or drinking! *You smell like (pick a name) today. You smelled like (pick a different name) yesterday.*

Yes, marriage does not mean that the two partners have to be joined at the hip. If it is challenging to maintain your individuality by staying together, staying apart is a good idea. But it is easier said than done – not because of children but the logistics of affordable housing! The current day work world helps a lot in this because many jobs have a travel component in them and it gives both a break from the monotony. It surprises me that we have still not been able to pry this entrenched institution of marriage from the fabric of our society.

Has it occurred to you that our jobs are another version of marriage? We lavish insane attention on our jobs. Make a lot of effort to appease our bosses. Find strategies to get along with our co-workers. Take on more load than we can bear for the collective success of the team. And finally, cheer and applaud the quarterly results because it has given birth to yet another seven-pound quarter to keep the business lineage procreating. And these marriages procreate every quarter.

All these years I have always kept this comparison to myself, but I will share it with you. Expecting a corporation to beat expectations each quarter is like expecting a woman to have an orgasm each time she has sex.

But then, what do you expect when we divorce the sciences from the arts? Like you say – it is happening in your alma mater. I have noticed that trend prevailing in India. I love how you say your son, the techie, is the deviant in your family when the world at large would consider him to be a solid young man making a valuable contribution to the technical world. *Vaise to baap zaraa teek nahi hai, magar beta first class!*

The single-minded pursuit of a conveyor belt education, coupled with a complete disregard for social sciences sucks away critical thinking and an examination of where we are in this world relative to the past and where we are headed. And I shudder to think where we are headed – what with the rewriting of history with a tarnished brush in every country.

... which brings us to Shaheen Bagh. When the whole issue started, I confess, I had to go back and do a lot of reading to understand why and how we got to where we are. We've only touched the tip of the iceberg on this. It is still lurking. And I tell you, it is like being on the Titanic not knowing what is coming around the bend.

I will rest my eyes a while on your words, to get my balance back:

Sometimes, only sometimes – for a fraction of a few seconds
I can see my reflection on my son's beautiful face
It is in those few moments of acute loneliness that I feel absolutely and irrevocably united with myself

Take care,
Tara

PS: (see below!)

Whoa, now! I finished replying to your previous letter and went out for a long bicycle ride, thinking I would send it out after I returned. Did I send it to you telepathically? Because I came back from the ride and found another letter waiting for me. One that talks about my bicycle rides in school! But more about that later.

No, I never asked you why you wrote to me. I took the airport interlude to be what it was. Two classmates meeting after years (and actually recognizing each other!) and sharing deep and intimate details in the anonymity of the airport because they don't expect to see one another again. In that way, airports are antiseptic spaces. And I always see them as transitional bridges – where we shed one persona and garb ourselves with another persona depending on where we are coming from or going to.

Whenever I used to transit through London Heathrow, I always found it fascinating to watch women getting off the flights from some of the

Middle East countries. Off would come the sleek, trendy, designer abaya, and get thrown casually over the arm, like some leather or cashmere coat. And under it, they would be wearing the tightest, barely breathable, figure hugging (or crotch hugging, as I used to think of it) trousers or jeans with airy, barely-there revealing tops. I loved that slip-off-show-off fashion show – the disappearance of the abaya-clad throw-on personality and the emergence of the real skin of the woman under it.

Back to the topic at hand...

When I got a letter from you twelve years after the airport run-in, I thought nothing of it. I read through it with mild curiosity. We do, after all, live in an age where we are constantly trying to reconnect with the past – some of us even going back to locate the doctor or midwife who birthed us. And the forming of social media groups among old schoolmates and the endless reminiscing is what clogs up the arteries of the internet these days.

Back in Montreal, I used to feel envious when my friends and colleagues waxed eloquent about their high school reunions, and about how their high school boyfriends commented that they still looked hot. If they were the wives, they went to check out if the girl who went to the senior prom with their husband still looked like they did in their high school yearbook photo. Of course, there were some who shunned these reunions like the plague.

If you had contacted me via social media where you were trying to get all the high school classmates together, you would have never heard from me. Since you took the time to write a letter, I replied promptly. A conversation between two adults, each giving time and thought to what the other has to say, is something that appealed to me.

I was surprised (and pleased) that our airport meeting found a place in your book *Pentacles*, and as I mentioned earlier, I bought a copy and read *Tara*. (confession: I have yet to read the rest of the book). I felt the mood in the ballad was a marker of where I was in my life at that point in time. And I was using it more to assess and analyse my journey in life since then. I will get to that in a bit.

So, while I did not ask you why you wrote to me, I was happy to reply. If there was a reason, I was willing to wait for you to tell me.

That said, your last letter is a bit disconcerting. I have not been blind to the various moods in your letters. I noticed a trend of despondency, self-loathing (is that the correct word?), introspection, self-flagellation, etc. and wondered if your conversations with me were a cry for help. Since you said you were continuing with the meds, I figured that you knew how to take care of your mental health. And when you mentioned you had lost interest in women, I figured our correspondence posed no threat to your marriage! You had mentioned writing a single word bored you to death, so I thought it was a good sign that you were able to write letters. And if it brought you out of your cage for a breath of fresh air, so much the better.

But I feel you are trying to project your worst side to me. Almost as if you are trying to say – *I am a horrible person, so don't reply to me, but please tell me if I love you. My wife thinks so, but I don't know.*

So I'm going to come right out and put it front and centre. Are you trying to, or asking me to, have an affair with you? Sorry for the bluntness – since we live several states apart, there are no visual clues – playing with hair, tossing of the head, leaning forward to place a light touch on the arm, and all the other subtle physical cues of the game. All I have are statements like this:

What does love mean for an almost old man like me today? I am very confused.

Today, to me, love is the soft incandescence of happiness. Do I feel like that towards you?

Like most of the boys in school, I was in love with you.

And then you dream of me cycling in slow motion to school, and wake up, deciding I was a signal in the darkness.

When I read that, my first thought was – what was the colour of our school uniform! As if that would make my legs more (or less) appealing in your dreams.

In a previous letter, you had mentioned that you were running out of first-hand experiences, so I'm wondering if a relationship with me is a new first-hand experience you were seeking? You don't seem to me like one of those men, but who am I to say? Like I said in an earlier letter, your words seem to me more of an internal struggle between what you are versus how you'd like to be perceived.

I am hoping that most of your thoughts were the coke (and the snorting of it) talking. But it concerns me that even during your tripping, you see me in my *teenage years cycling in slow motion towards a reddish moon.*

If I am mistaken in your intentions, you can come down on me like a ton of bricks and correct me. It will not cause any embarrassment to me for overthinking the situation, and neither will I stop writing to you. I have embraced the western world's casualness towards discussing these matters openly. And I also feel you have a need of a friend, who does not scuttle away while you keep exposing more and more of your (un)desirable side!

Now, back to your ballad *Tara*. Like I said I was using it more to assess and analyse my journey in life since then. When we ran into each other at the airport, I was at a low point in my life. And I felt very much like the girl in the movie I was trying to make – the one who was imprisoned in a dungeon for eighteen years and does not know the language of the world when she emerges.

I was somewhat at the crossroads. Having left a country when I was barely twenty years old, having lived a very unconventional life, did I have it in me to wake up on the other side and rebuild my life, from the detritus of an old one. Or should I go back to my twenty-year-old persona and grow her up instead in a place like India and see who would emerge without the Montreal experience. The latter seemed easier – if I could only remember who she was and if I had the energy to groom her into being. But the years outside India had left a lot of memory gaps, and instead of embarking on a tedious remake, I hauled the woman I had become back to the land of my birth.

I was prepared for it to be hard. But, boy, was I underprepared for how painstakingly hard it would be! In your ballad you have written:

> *But when I lost hope of survival in a foreign land,*
> *And the moral strength to continue in absolute darkness,*
> *That comes with the frenzy of silence and isolation,*
> *It was my land (to whose air, food and language I belonged)*
> *That beckoned me in my dreams sending me streams of light and warmth,*
> *(Embracing me in its delicate haze) as if telling me softly,*
> *I could survive here with a chance.*

In the beginning, if only you knew how feeble that beckoning was in reality, how the *streams of light and warmth* were actually the bright, burning spotlights of judgement and scorn – that will give you an idea of what my initial two attempts at returning to the land of my birth were like. When we met at the airport, Pondicherry was a distant glimmer of hope. I was still reeling from my previous two attempts, so I was despondent and morbid.

Since then, (a dozen years, right?) I have found my place both in body and soul. I am rooted in the new life I have created for myself in Pondicherry. I now believe *I could survive here with a chance.*

Back in your ballad,

it was true that I said

Silence is the pinnacle of isolation; it kills us from inside.
When you have been abandoned by the soul that you love most dearly,
You plunge into absolute isolation and absolute silence.

The silence that fills my days now is no longer one of isolation. It is a companionable silence, a friendly silence, a willing companion who walks by my side. Not one that is goaded and dragged along, kicking and screaming...

it was true that I said:

Each time I had to crawl up an abyss,
Similar to an unending shaft of a coal mine:
Breathless and infinitely depressed.

Today I am breathless, not because I have crawled up an abyss, clawing my way out by my fingernails. I am breathless as I have found myself right where I've always been – within myself.

it was true that I said:

But when I lost hope of survival in a foreign land,
And the moral strength to continue in absolute darkness,

I am in a foreign land, albeit the land of my birth. But my moral strength is no longer floundering in absolute darkness. It embraces whatever light shines on it. Sometimes it is a bright welcoming light, sometimes it is the absence of light. I survive it – gracefully and in peace.

I think you may have noticed it in my replies to your letters. Except for a few lapses, the mood and tone of my replies are far removed from what you remember of your airport companion. And I think that frustrates you because you want me to come at your words with my fangs bared! *Tara, what sort of animal am I?* And I am happy to be your foil – bring it on! Just so we know on which battlefield we stand and what (non)weapons we bring...

Love,
Tara

March 11th, 2022
Kolkata

Dear Tara,

Thank you for your wonderful letter!

When you say: *What I'd like to see is accountability and taking personal responsibility for their acts*; I agree with you. I completely agree with you. But you cannot club Jeffrey Epstein with Woody Allen, Roman Polanski, and Kevin Spacey.

If mankind has spent so many resources to understand the minds of serial killers, then why should we not understand the minds of serial sexual offenders?

Tara, as I stand today, I think I am incapable of loving and being loved. I have wasted my life to that extent.

The slogan on my flag reads as follows:

I want to be your friend. I want you to become my friend. I want to stand beside you. I want you to stand beside me. I do not want to colonize you. I do not want you to colonize me. I want to be free. I want you to be free. I want our friendship to challenge all formal and structured relationships.

The war and the climate of war all around us are devastating me. A few days back, I wrote a poem, titled: *An Old Man Rising*; it goes as follows:

The smell of ashes
Fills up my abraded soul
Sitting alongside the yellow river, on its banks,

The smell of ashes
From distant lands
Traverse serpentile invisible in the air
Choke our glands, and nerves

War games, played very long, have paved ways to wars
Anybody can go to war now
Drop bombs, shoot missiles, and go nuclear
Such is the way

In my youth we planned silent wars against the wars of
oligarchs
Nothing has stopped the truant war games of the oligarchs
And, now silly wars, they have played war games for
too long
Now they need new wars

Life seems futile sitting lonely alongside the yellow
river, on its banks,
With choked glands, and nerves

Remembering the wars that happened in my lifetime
The Bangladesh war
The Iran – Iraq war, protracted over years,
The Iraq – Kuwait war
Afghanistan crumbled to the ground
Syria crumbled to the ground
The Kargil war in between

Now, Russia attacks Ukraine on whims and fancy
Ukraine left abandoned by the NATO powers
Yet, its citizens roaming the smoking landscapes
strident, and strong

I rise up on the riverbank, remembering other wars
Smoking a cigarette

Other wars that the oligarchs play on our daily lives
Killing us, mauling us, humiliating us, insulting us

The smell of ashes enervates my bloodstream in slow motion
By the side of the yellow river

Remembering my past lines:

Before I passed out and became sediment of ashes I saw
a dream
of billion coffins made of trees, metal and hydrocarbon
fibers
carrying unbundled skeletons of men, women, children and
babies ballooning up in a smoke-filled sky.

Yesterday night, I could not sleep at all in spite having taken four tablets of Lonazep 0.5 mg. I am feeling sleepy now. I will take your leave. Before going, I want you to take note of a very favorite poem by my favorite poet Osip Emilevich Mandelstam:

What shall I do with this body they gave me,
so much my own, so intimate with me?

For being alive, for the joy of calm breath,
tell me, who should I bless?

I am the flower, and the gardener as well,
and am not solitary, in earth's cell.

My living warmth, exhaled, you can see,
on the clear glass of eternity.

A pattern set down,
until now, unknown.

Breath evaporates without trace,
but form no one can deface.

Bye bye,

Love,
Sandy

Post Scriptum: *Expecting a corporation to beat expectations each quarter is like expecting a woman to have an orgasm each time she has sex.* - I like it. I like it very much. To be frank, in my time, I have been very, very careful about the woman's pleasure, I was pleasuring with.

March 15th, 2022
Pondicherry

Dear Sandy,

I know there are a lot of deep talks we must have, based on your letter, but please, please allow me to share some exciting news with you.

Apropos our discussion about Marilyn Monroe, I came across a news item yesterday about a letter that John Steinbeck wrote to Marilyn Monroe. I couldn't believe it at first, because it seemed so unlikely. So, I did some poking around, and it is highly likely that he did write it. Even if he didn't, I'd like to think that he did. I have placed the letter here as it was reproduced in the article I read. Something tells me you will share in my excitement.

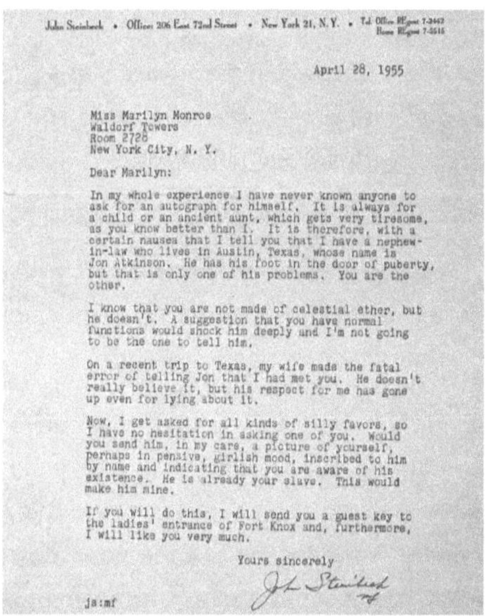

John Steinbeck • Office: 206 East 72nd Street • New York 21, N.Y. • Tel. Office: REgent 7-2442
Home REgent 7-4545

April 28, 1955

Miss Marilyn Monroe
Waldorf Towers
Room 2728
New York City, N. Y.

Dear Marilyn:

In my whole experience I have never known anyone to ask for an autograph for himself. It is always for a child or an ancient aunt, which gets very tiresome, as you know better than I. It is therefore, with a certain nausea that I tell you that I have a nephew-in-law who lives in Austin, Texas, whose name is Jon Atkinson. He has his foot in the door of puberty, but that is only one of his problems. You are the other.

I know that you are not made of celestial ether, but he doesn't. A suggestion that you have normal functions would shock him deeply and I'm not going to be the one to tell him.

On a recent trip to Texas, my wife made the fatal error of telling Jon that I had met you. He doesn't really believe it, but his respect for me has gone up even for lying about it.

Now, I get asked for all kinds of silly favors, so I have no hesitation in asking one of you. Would you send him, in my care, a picture of yourself, perhaps in pensive, girlish mood, inscribed to him by name and indicating that you are aware of his existence. He is already your slave. This would make him mine.

If you will do this, I will send you a guest key to the ladies' entrance of Fort Knox and, furthermore, I will like you very much.

Yours sincerely

John Steinbeck

ja:mf

Do you think Monroe sent a picture of herself to Steinbeck's nephew? For that, we will have to find out if the guest key to the ladies' entrance of Fort Knox was ever found in her possession, among her belongings after she died! And why would Monroe ever go to Fort Knox? That was not her playing ground. If a key was found, I'm sure common belief would have been that it belonged to some secret hideout in the White House.

I would like to think that she did not send her picture because she didn't want Steinbeck's nephew looking up her skirt from his bed. How would she ever face Steinbeck if she ran into him outside the ladies' entrance of Fort Knox? Would she lose her *key* privileges?

And now I'm ready to move on to your letter, where you have given me a flag instead of the spare keys. Is it a white flag raised in surrender, or as used in Canadian football – an orange penalty flag thrown to contest, challenge or draw attention to an infraction? I'm guessing it is the latter – *I want our friendship to challenge all formal and structured relationships.* So be it, so be it! I am free and I will not be colonized – so we are both on the same page. You may now lower your flag!

Again, sorry for the bluntness in asking *are you trying to, or asking me to, have an affair with you?* (...she says, while she slips out of her clothes and watches with amusement as he throws down the orange penalty flag... again)

While you did not come down on me like a ton of bricks, you, at least, showed me where the bricks are stored. Stored behind your flag, so that you can lob them at challengers and duck!

Besides the war within yourself, you (and all of us) are also dealing with all the wars during our lifetime – in your poem *An Old Man Rising.* I still haven't found the poem I promised you a few letters back, but your poem reminded me of a few poems by Naomi Shihab Nye, an American-born daughter of a Palestinian refugee.

This one titled *For Mohammed Zeid of Gaza, Age 15* is about a stray
bullet.

There is no stray bullet, sirs.

...

So don't gentle it, please.

...

But this bullet had no innocence, did not
wish anyone well, you can't tell us otherwise
by naming it mildly, this bullet was never the friend
of life, should not be granted immunity
by soft saying—friendly fire, straying death-eye,
why have we given the wrong weight to what we do?

Mohammed, Mohammed, deserves the truth.
This bullet had no secret happy hopes,
it was not singing to itself with eyes closed
under the bridge.

Another one, about the leader of the free world, who was not charged
for war crimes, is titled *He Said EYE-RACK*

...

...

He said, "We are
against the lawless men who
rule your country, not you." Tell that
to the mother, the sister, the bride,
the proud boy, the peanut-seller,
the librarian careful with her shelves.
The teacher, the spinner, the sweeper,
the invisible village, the thousands of people

with laundry and bread, the ants tunneling
through the dirt.

There are several others about war, but these two speak to me in the light of this current conflict. I thought I would share some snippets with you, instead of the entire poem.

I am not a newsmaker, but a film maker. And one of the drawbacks I see in this garb is that I am unable to talk in staccato beats about events as they are happening. Gets traumatic. Film making allows you to process and decide how you want history to be told. Again, not necessarily a good thing – we are all seeing how history can be remade and recast in different moulds depending on the weapons of the maker. Either way, we are screwed. And so is the world.

Which brings me to another poem by Naomi Shihab Nye titled *The Day.*

I missed the day
on which it was said
others should not have
certain weapons, but we could.
Not only could, but should,
          and do.
I missed that day.
Was I sleeping?

...

A snippet from the poem, but you can replace 'others' by any disenfranchised group, and 'certain weapons' by the artillery we use to disenfranchise them, and you have described every authoritarian country in the world. Another reason why this poem is so relevant in the current world.

And yes, to quote from your letter:

What shall I do with this body they gave me,

Love
Tara

PS: Only a postscript in your letter for my brilliant comparison? I'm glad you liked it, though. I always used to imagine all the analysts on the quarterly earnings call hanging on to every word to figure out if the company's performance met market expectations. Beat market expectations? Underperform? Did they? Didn't they? What factors are they blaming? Certain acquisitions? So much pressure! So much pressure! And all of them falling back, panting, sweating – was it good for you – or – its okay, I'm sure it'll be better next time. With this, I bid you adieu!

PPS: And yes, I agree to removing Jeffrey Epstein from the Woody Allen, Roman Polanski, and Kevin Spacey club, if you allow me to put him in another club with a fellow offender – our colonizer who is hiding behind his mother's Kohinoor diamond.

March 16th, 2022
Kolkata

Dear Tara,

I am truly vexed by John Steinbeck's letter to Marilyn Monroe dated April 28, 1955, and your comments thereafter.

Am I asking you to have an affair with me? Affair is too pale a word for me to be having at my age. I need something thicker and more viscous.

We have lived many kinds of relationships that have caged us. Rarely, do we live a relationship that frees us? These relationships are lived on the jagged edges of an abyss. I am very confused about what I really want. The fact is, I love writing to you and baring my soul. Possibly, this will heal me. I am deeply broken and fractured from the inside. *Do I need your help to get my act together?* I would say you are a signal in the darkness.

When I look back at my past, I can see an unending desert with no hint of an oasis. When I look into my future, I can see you as a signal in the darkness. My family is like scattering radially like free electrons moving into multifarious directions.

That I do not feel rooted, that I do not feel attached is another disease with me.

How can you not remember the school dress! The girls' dress was grey skirt above the knee line, white shirt with the school emblem stitched on to the left breast pocket, blue tie with white stripes in the middle, and red blazer with the school emblem stitched on to the left breast pocket. This was the dress for the winters.

Maybe I would like to walk by your side along the seafront during sunrise in Pondicherry. I do not know, possibly I would like to put my head on your bosom and tell you a banal story of my childhood or maybe even a fairy tale.

Seriously – I want you to come down to Kolkata for a weekend, or you invite me to Pondicherry.

The excerpts from the poems of Naomi Shihab Nye are brilliant. In 2002, I had travelled to Damascus from Amman around midnight by road; the taxi was driven by a Palestinian, who sang songs of freedom during our journey, very similar to a Kashmiri driver, who had taken me from Srinagar to Kargil in 2005 and sang us songs of *azaadi*.

I was thinking the other day – my generation has witnessed and experienced some of the most time-defining events and changes in the history of mankind. I thought of listing down a few of them:

1. Bhopal Gas Tragedy.
2. Chernobyl Disaster.
3. Introduction of Plastic Money.
4. Introduction of mass computerization and the Internet.
5. Introduction of Robotics, Machine Learning, Artificial/Applied Intelligence, Internet of Things and Internet of Services.
6. Introduction of Cellphones.
7. Cloud Computing.
8. Quantum Computing.

9. Genome Decoding.
10. Creation of Iraq – Iran – Israel – Palestine Conflict Zone.
11. Rise of Political Islam growing on the nexus between the CIA, Saudi Arabia and Pakistan.
12. Growth of Economic Globalization as a phenomenon.
13. 9/11.
14. Decimation of Afghanistan, Iraq and Syria.
15. Rise of extreme nationalist forces in the second decade of the 21st Century worldwide.
16. Emergence of HIV.
17. Possibility of Gene Alteration and Mutation.
18. Stem Cell Technology.
19. Covid-19.
20. Possible onset of World War III.

For each one of them, huge tomes would have to be written to understand them in their entirety. The above list is only indicative, and not complete. You can add to or subtract from the list, according to your wish.

Nowadays, I feel very tired. Today I will end with a poem by Anna Akhamatova.

VII
THE VERDICT

The word landed with a stony thud
Onto my still-beating breast.
Nevermind, I was prepared,
I will manage with the rest.

I have a lot of work to do today;
I need to slaughter memory,
Turn my living soul to stone
Then teach myself to live again...

But how. The hot summer rustles
Like a carnival outside my window;
I have long had this premonition
Of a bright day and a deserted house.
[22 June 1939. Summer. Fontannyi Dom (4)]

From Requiem by Anna Akhamatova

Bye bye,

Love,
Sandy

March 19ᵗʰ, 2022
Kolkata

Dear Tara,

Today, I would like to tell you a few things.

I always wanted to be like my *Baba*: self-made, independent, and ferociously courageous. He stayed alone in a men's hostel in Kolkata during his under graduation, post-graduation, and his LLB. He paid his dues by conducting tuition classes for higher-secondary and undergraduate students. He got married to my mother in 1964 in Kolkata, and immediately after that, he started earning. He took care of his brother financially who was into full-time leftist politics then. *Baba* was a man driven by a passion for visiting new places, although he passionately loved the nearness to high mountains the most. *Baba* lost his *Ma* at the age of twelve. And, lost his *Baba* at the age of twenty-two due to the aggressive ravages of diabetes Type-2. In more ways than one, my *Ma* turned out to be his only companion although he had a wide array of friends and relatives, who he always took care of at the slightest hint.

To top it all, *Baba* was a wonderful storyteller. He could attract children through his storytelling skills of Sukumar Ray, and children's stories written by Rabindranath Tagore, and Hans Christian Andersen. He pampered me a lot. But I think I could never become a man like him because of his splurging habits.

Although there has been a great difference of opinion between me and my *Ma*, I do not think I have been a good son to my parents. For this, I repent a lot nowadays. There is something inside me that stops me from becoming the kind of person that I want to be.

Civil Engineering, for which I took training at Jadavpur University, never reached the soul of my passion until I was in a difficult spot in my profession. It was then that I came to understand that Civil Engineering deals with all the indeterminate variables of nature like soil, environment, wind, earthquakes, etc. It was also through Civil Engineering that I could reach the amorphous nature of our lives. I fell in love with Civil Engineering as much as I was in love with Leo Tolstoy or T S Elliot. My parents taught me the beauty of interdisciplinary education. I thank them wholeheartedly for that: a wonderful journey comprising the pleasures of reading, writing, watching movies, travelling, pursuing interests in natural sciences, and technological subjects.

My son, who is a Geo-technical expert, and my daughter, who is an independent film maker on environmental issues have inherited these traits from me and Niharika. I think my children have turned out to be self-centered, self-obsessed, and self-indulgent like me, and, who can I blame for this except myself!

If I have come close to loving anybody, without going into the definitions of love, it is Niharika. However, at the end of the day, we are incompatible for the simple reason that our likes, dislikes, and interests are very different from each other. Yet, we stick together without talking to each other for months! I do not know how long this can continue.

I have green eyes because my *Ma* had green eyes. The question is from where did my *Ma* get green eyes? From my grandmother. My grandmother's grandmother was married to a Civil Engineer, who graduated from Government Engineering College, Howrah with distinction and a gold medal in 1892. He was posted at a site in Orissa where the massive Cuttack railway bridge was under construction, where he was designated as the Superintending Engineer. He reported to a Portuguese Jew [in a British Monolith!] who had a pair of wonderful green eyes.

My grandmother's grandmother was an expert in the *Meera Bai* tradition of *kirtans* and *bhajans,* which this Portuguese Jew grew in love with gradually over weekend dinners hosted by the Superintending Engineer at his house, who was quite oblivious of the fact that a secret relationship was developing over *kirtans* and *bhajans.* The Superintending Engineer concentrated on the bridge and the Chief Engineer concentrated on my grandmother's grandmother. A secret liaison blossomed between them. A year and a half later, my grandmother's mother was born with a pair of sparkling green eyes. I forgot to tell you that my grandmother's grandmother had a pair of deep black eyes.

The point to tell you is, that I have something Jewish in me apart from the fact that my father and his clan belong to the *Vaishya* community. Sometimes I think what kind of a merchant am I? Am I a merchant of unending unhappiness?

I would like to end this letter today with a poem written by *Federico Garcia Lorca* from his anthology titled: *City That Does Not Sleep.*

Another day
we will watch the preserved butterflies rise from the dead

and still walking through a country of gray sponges and silent boats
we will watch our ring flash and roses spring from our tongue.
Careful! Be careful! Be careful!
The men who still have marks of the claw and the thunderstorm,
and that boy who cries because he has never heard of the invention
of the bridge,
or that dead man who possesses now only his head and a shoe,
we must carry them to the wall where the iguanas and the snakes
are waiting,
where the bear's teeth are waiting,
where the mummified hand of the boy is waiting,
and the hair of the camel stands on end with a violent blue shudder.

Bye bye,

Love,
Sandy

March 22nd, 2022
Pondicherry

Dear Sandy,

Vexed? Surely not with Steinbeck's letter to Monroe? I thought that discovery was delightful, though unexpected. While I waited for your reply, I dug around some more. The letter was in Monroe's archives – she left a major part of her estate to Lee Strasberg, her acting coach. Strasberg's second wife, Anna, inherited the letter.

The reporter located Steinbeck's nephew at his home in Alabama, where he lives with his wife. He is – hold your breath – a retired minister! If memory serves him right, he didn't receive a picture from Marilyn Monroe – which makes me think – getting a letter from Steinbeck was a big deal for Monroe, since she kept his letter among her archives.

Talking of archives, look at what you brought out from yours – the exact details of our school uniform down to the emblem on the left breast pocket. I'm sure you will remember the design of the emblem, too! Maybe I have some school pictures stored away in my boxes that may have jogged my memory. Along with the poem I've been promising to share with you. Dammit, where did I put that poem?

Vexed? Even as I am adapting to your flag and adjusting to the contours of your definitions? I thought my *So be it* summed up my response. In case it didn't, here it is – I see your flag and I raise you one.

Affair is too pale a word? *Hookup* is too juvenile a word. Remember, I come from the land of '*Your place or mine?*' And the word doesn't matter. I can relate to the dense, opaque darkness of being broken and fractured on the inside. I have not-so-distant memories of being there myself. If writing to me opens the door for you to bare your soul and lighten your load, I will continue replying.

Me coming to Kolkata? Huh? That is your playing ground, Sandy. Sandy's sandbox, so to speak. I'll leave that city to you and your family. You could consider coming to Pondicherry. You said you've been here before, so you probably know as much of the town as I do, and also how to get here. We can promenade down Goubert Avenue, (or Beach Road, as it is called) not just during sunrise, but sunset also, though it does get crowded in the evenings. If we finish our walk before 7:30 am, we would be in the traffic-free window. Or start the evening walk after 6 pm. As for putting your head on my bosom, get real, man – is that *really* the time to share childhood stories? (... she says, shaking her head)

Who knows, by the end of your visit, I may have been downgraded from the *signal in the darkness* to *that dot at the bottom of the abyss.* There is a huge leap between the schoolgirl cycling to school in her winter uniform to the woman I am today. Be warned!

(a few hours later)

Just got back from a long bike ride to clear my head. (Do you bike?) And found another letter from you. I was planning to continue our discussion but will switch tracks and move to your latest letter.

I find it so heartening to hear that your parents gave you a well-rounded education. Something that the educational institutions these days would do very well to emulate. Sometimes I am appalled by the tone-deaf discourses I see here among the highly *educated.* And I'm not even sure if the teaching staff is qualified to impart a multidisciplinary curriculum.

If you've passed on the same disciplinary exposure to your children, why do you think they are self-centred, self-obsessed, and self-indulgent? Do you think they are picking up vibes of discord between their parents and retreating to protect themselves?

Though, to be frank, I've heard of this *living together without talking to each other for months* from other long-married couples. I guess there is a complacency that creeps in when you see the same face day after day across the dining table or in the shared bathroom mirror or even facing each other in bed. Some embrace it like a lovable well-worn, but thread bare shawl, while others would want to revamp and bring in the new. You seem to belong to the latter. Does Niharika belong to the former?

Wait... what?? I had to read the grandmother's grandmother information a few times to unravel that and get a picture in my mind. So... your grandmother's grandmother (let's call her GG) was married to the Superintending Engineer of the Cuttack railway bridge construction (let's call him SE). He reported to a man with green eyes. (I don't want to call him GE because that sounds too much like an appliance – GE refrigerator or something like that. Let's call him MG – Man with Green eyes) And while SE was building a bridge, MG was building the lineage of your family with GG. How intriguing! And what happened when a baby girl was born with green eyes? Did the green-eyed monster (pun intended) raise its head in SE? Did GG have other children? With non-green eyes? My camera is going click-click-click here.

This GG part is more interesting than the *merchant of unending unhappiness*? Because you – *the merchant* – are in the here-and-now and we can always knit that one back together. Do I sound unsympathetic? Or uncaring? Isn't it amazing how we are captivated by anecdotes from the past, especially when it doesn't involve us personally? Is it because we can't change it – it happened – and we can't change the facts, but we can change the lens through which we look at it.

With the present – like you being the *merchant of unending unhappiness* – it is happening and there are ways in which we can try to change that outcome. So, we don't find it intriguing, but more like a project – something to be worked on. Okay, now I truly sound unsympathetic.

Next!

You told me in an earlier letter that your father's family had migrated to Nabadwip in the Nadia district from the Manikganj sub-division in Dacca, Bangladesh when he was about ten years old. Piecing scraps of information together, I'm calculating that he lost his mother a couple of years after the move. Did it have anything to do with the trials and tribulations of the move? And he lost his father about twelve years after that. I know they got married young back in the day – did your grandfather live long enough to see your father married? What happened to the memoir your father was writing?

I don't have much by way of these stories. My parents died in an accident – much of their history died with them. I suppose if I lived in India, I would have spent time stitching together the fabric of their lives by reaching out to extended family members. But their lives fell victim to the only-child-living-abroad-rushing-to-the funeral narrative. I was too shaken up by the complications of arranging a funeral for two accident victims (or roadkill, as I later called it) in India, to worry about the artefacts of their lives. Not to speak of climbing the mounds of paperwork to settle their meagre belongings, Luckily, there was not much to wrap up – he was a music teacher, as you mentioned in your ballad. All I had was my memories of the Beatles tunes he taught me to play on the piano. So, I had them play *Let It Be* loud enough at the cremation to drown out the chants. Many of them put it down to the laments of a deranged and grieving daughter. Mother Mary at a Punjabi cremation – it brings a smile to my lips even today, but I am convinced my father loved it. And my mother loved my father, so she would have been shaking her head indulgently at the father-daughter duo.

Here are the lyrics, though I'm sure you have it memorized:

When I find myself in times of trouble, Mother Mary comes to me
Speaking words of wisdom, let it be
And in my hour of darkness she is standing right in front of me
Speaking words of wisdom, let it be
Let it be, let it be, let it be, let it be
Whisper words of wisdom, let it be
And when the brokenhearted people living in the world agree
There will be an answer, let it be
For though they may be parted, there is still a chance that they will see
There will be an answer, let it be
Let it be, let it be, let it be, let it be
There will be an answer, let it be
Let it be, let it be, let it be, let it be
Whisper words of wisdom, let it be
Let it be, let it be, let it be, let it be
Whisper words of wisdom, let it be
And when the night is cloudy there is still a light that shines on me
Shine until tomorrow, let it be
I wake up to the sound of music, Mother Mary comes to me
Speaking words of wisdom, let it be
Let it be, let it be, let it be, yeah, let it be
There will be an answer, let it be
Let it be, let it be, let it be, yeah, let it be
Whisper words of wisdom, let it be

Today, I will leave you with this.

Love

Tara

March 23rd, 2022
Kolkata

Dear Tara,

Am I hallucinating the slow dance of infinite stars?

To be in a constant state of sadness simmering at the corner of your soul is a disease. Melancholia. Psychiatrists and therapists have not been able to identify what kick-started this in me. It kick-started in my adolescence. My sister was born nine years after I was born. I was very happy with her birth. But I lost *Ma* to my sister. Even at an early age of six, I dreamt of living with *Ma* alone among the mountains when I would grow up. As we grew up, *Ma* found it easier to mentor my sister as I was a terribly disobedient boy. (Her mentorship is one of the reasons that she has become so successful in her work. I take great pride in her work because I love her very much, which I have not been able to demonstrate till now.) The rift widened. I became a drifter. I was serious about nothing. Nothing at all. I was not sincere. I was not honest. I pursued easy ideas or pretended to pursue an idea while I was actually idling away my time. I talked big. Melancholia set in, in a comprehensible pattern, in love at the age of eighteen when I was ditched by a very beautiful girl. I was so self-absorbed and selfish that I did not labour enough to keep my friendships and would avoid them later. A mood of futility had set in.

With growing age and many ups-and-downs, I have become more alone and my melancholia has spread through my body.

This growing melancholia did many good things - it made me more sincere and truthful; it made me more creative; it made me lucid, and it made me feel like one with the many unhappy souls in the world - the disadvantaged, the disenfranchised, the oppressed, and victims of injustice and irrationality. However, the surprising part is I did nothing for them. Slowly, my inaction and cowardice enhanced the intensity of my melancholia.

I wrote to my son on March 13, 2019:

I think with age I am getting very cynical because of the following two reasons:

1. *The political climate of irrationality, injustice, hate and violence in India.*

2. *Nepotism and politicking at my workplace are the two most significant parameters - in place of ethics, hard work, innovation and imagination - for growth.*

These two factors are encapsulating my mind and soul with very negative thoughts.

Sometimes I think the two escapes could be - beautiful landscapes and rich conversations.

Apart from earning money, what do I do? I read classics. I watch movies. I read news from all across the world. I listen to music. I think and think and think. Like riding a helix. And, I write.

I have never done anything that makes me proud of myself. I want to change my life. I want to change my life before I die. I want to die honourably in my own eyes.

The tribals in our heartland forests are doing a great duty to nature - they are the ecological watchdogs of our forests. The mining barons, politicians of all hues and justices are conniving to throw them out of these forests. I think it will be a good idea to get lost amidst these jungles. How tough and life-bending is it for a man who cannot stand tropical heat, the sight of insects and dirt, is used to a home diet and water, not used to life without the Internet and many other things to take this step?

I believe firmly, that it is this - these landscapes and the conversations there - which can heal me. I have never dived inside a rough sea ever. I have to take a plunge somewhere in my life.

Two enduring memories of *Ma* are:

1. Until the age of seven, after returning from school and having had my lunch, I would wrap around *Ma* in bed and sleep in her bosom and womb. The peace that I felt during those moments was unbelievable.

2. After my sister was born when I was nine years old, my bed wetting habit increased in frequency. When I was in Standard IX, one night when I had wet my bed, and the chill of the mattress touched my back, I could hear *Ma* screaming, howling, and later, crying. I did not know what to do except continue shivering in the stillness of the night. My bed wetting habit vanished when I was midway in Standard X.

When I was in Standard I, I would read stories by Lila Majumdar, and one night I dreamt of becoming a writer and living in the mountains with *Ma*. Destiny had something else in store for me.

I must compliment you for your research on John Steinbeck and Marilyn Monroe.

I will definitely come down to Pondicherry. Biking down Goubert Avenue is a wonderful idea.

Baba lost his *Ma* a few years after the move from Bangladesh. It could have been due to the trials and tribulations of the move. My grandfather did not live long enough to see *Baba* married. *Baba*, presently, is lost in his ideas of natural justice and has temporarily stopped writing his memoir.

Do you remember Ramesh Chatly and Navdeep Loomba with whom I used to hang out in school? The other day I came across a journal entry of our school years, which reads as follows:

Possibly it was at the end of 1978 or 1979 (I was in Class VII or VIII and quite unaware of the turmoil the country was going through at that time) when I was introduced to the Video Cassette Player/Recorder (Akai make) at Ramesh Chatly's residence in Ludhiana. Ramesh, Navdeep and I were great buddies in school. With the excuse of playing cricket or studying, Navdeep and I would go to Ramesh's house and play Monopoly (Ramesh introduced us to this game) or watch a pot-boiler Hindi movie, whichever was available. In those days the Esquire company of Singapore made movie cassettes and they were of very good quality. Gradually, playing Monopoly and watching pot-boiler Hindi movies in the cool confines of Ramesh's home became an addiction and we no longer paid any attention to studies or cricket. Before or after these sessions, we would go out and devour a lot of street food that played havoc with our digestive system. Whenever I remember those days now, it seems all these happened only a few years back shrouded inside a yellow mystery bag.

Last night, I listened to *Let It Be* on Apple music around ten-to-twelve times. The song is swirling in my soul right now.

Bye bye,

Love,
Sandy

March 28th, 2022
Pondicherry

Dear Sandy,

Hearing you talk about your angst about losing your mother's attention makes me glad I was an only child. Though there have been many, many, many times I have wished for a brother and a sister. Yes, and. Not or. This feeling became one of abject despair when I lost my parents and had no one to share common memories with, no one to check if a particular incident happened or if it was a figment of my imagination. I guess it hit me harder because my parents didn't leave me one after the other, didn't live up to old age when one can swap out rosy memories with the daily concerns of failing body parts when one transitions to the child becoming the adult in the relationship.

Between your letter to your son in 2019 and today, nothing has changed, has it? For the better, I mean. If at all, things have become worse, haven't they? Sometimes the rhetoric becomes so bizarre and dystopian that one suspects one's own sanity and thinks one lives in an alternate reality. In fact, during the pandemic years, I found myself going back and reading Orwell's 1984 a couple of times. There is no way left to die honourably anymore, because we have all been living in this skewed reality and even our small efforts at sanity do not absolve us from the sins of being eyewitnesses to whatever is happening. So don't look to me for healing. I am also one of the walking wounded.

But don't let this put you off from visiting Pondicherry.

I don't normally cycle down Goubert Avenue during the day with all the traffic, but decided to check it out, after my suggestion to you to visit Pondicherry, and wanted to picture us either walking or biking along the avenue.

It was crowded – and I took a breather at one of the cafes that dot that avenue – to get away from traffic.

I ran into a woman I know. We do stuff together off and on. Sometimes we meet while biking and continue together for the rest of the ride. Sometimes we see a play or a movie together. Or even a music performance. She stopped and joined me at the café, commenting that she had never seen me biking at that time of day. Over coffee and sandwiches, I told her that I was scoping out the area from the point of view of a visitor.

She was quite amused, since (her words) she thought I lived a solitary life, happy with my own company. I shrugged and said that I had reconnected with an old school mate who now lived in Kolkata. Her reaction surprised me. I didn't expect her to get all animated at the mention of Kolkata. Turns out she is from Kolkata, or Calcutta as it was called when she grew up there. And now she spends her time between Kolkata and Pondicherry. Family commitments, maybe, but I didn't ask. So, that's where she was during the weeks and months that I never ran into her.

We veered off into other topics, but when we parted, I suggested that we meet when you come here for a visit. Seemanti (that's her name) said she would like that very much and looked forward to it.

So that is one more thing we can do when you come here.

Love
Tara

April 7th, 2022
Pondicherry

Dear Sandy,

I got so used to expecting your replies within a week, that this ten-day delay is quite unlike you. Is everything okay?

I'm skipping the order in replies because I wanted to tell you to add a few more events to your list:

Bombay riots in 1993

26/11 attacks in Bombay

Sri Lankan Civil War

Tsunami in 2004

I'm sure we are leaving out a lot more. Though localized, some events did have impacts that resonated across several countries.

Yes, we can tell people – *I was there when this happened* – but who would we tell it to? Babies born on 9/11 would have crossed twenty years last September. So, we have to tell them, and everyone born after that – *it was before your time*. They would never be able to comprehend what that did to the world and what it led to. When one thinks of this, we realize how insignificant we are in the whole scheme of things.

Boy, I'm getting morbid! Is it because of the anxiety of not having received your letter? I think I have to print your slogan and pin it above my desk.

I do not want to colonize you. I do not want you to colonize me.

With a deep breath,

Love
Tara

April 17th, 2022
Pondicherry

Dear Sandy,

This is getting curiouser and curiouser – to quote Alice in Wonderland.
I can understand one letter going astray, but two? Did I bump into
the *I do not know how long this can continue* from your earlier letters?
I didn't think it was in reference to our correspondence, but who
knows…

I don't want to sound like a needy teenager, so I'll keep this short and
hope that the vagaries of the mail system sort themselves out.

Love
Tara

May 5th, 2022
Pondicherry

Dearest Sandy,

Ah, okay. Now I understand.

I decided to read *Pentacles* while I waited for your reply. Sooner or later, you would catch up with your mail.

If you remember, I had only read the ballad *Tara* till date. I read *Tara* again, and idly turned to the previous piece. It seemed like the stories in the book were not connected in any way, so I worked my way from the back and finally came up to the first story *New Life*. The reading was going swimmingly well – until the phone rang and the protagonist picked it up.

I stopped reading.

I flung the book on the table and rushed out of the house and ran – not as if I was one among many runners on Beach Road, but as if something was chasing me and I had to run faster to outpace that *something*.

Several hours later, I returned home, exhausted, limping, and breathless. I avoided my study for the rest of the day.

In the days that followed, I went into a frenzy of cleaning, as if by clearing my physical spaces, I was also clearing my mental spaces.

After a couple of days, I entered my study since I needed some papers. *Pentacles* lay askew exactly where I had dropped it and fled from the house. I used another book to push it away from the papers I needed and left the study. As if it was a pile of smouldering embers.

I could not avoid going into my study indefinitely. And I could not pretend that there was nothing more to read after the late-night phone call the protagonist gets. There was more to the story *New Life*. So, I geared myself up for a late night read, and fortified the path ahead with copious amounts of gin and tonic, and plunged in.

Enter Seemanti.

Seemanti? Seemanti who divides her time between Kolkata and Pondicherry due to family commitments.

Coincidences abound in fiction, but in real life – only very rarely.

After the grandfather clock (yes, one of my quaint possessions that I shipped back here from Montreal) welcomed the midnight hour, I closed the book and rubbed my tired eyes. After tossing and turning in bed, I sat up and went back to reading our letters over again, in case I had missed something. Another part of your life, maybe, that you had tucked in among the poetry or narrative descriptions? All along I thought you were giving me details of your life – the one you live now – and in return, I was sharing details of my life. But there was never any mention of anyone by the name of Seemanti.

Seemingly innocuous, right? One would have thought so. But the only reason I can find for your silence was this sentence in my letter: *I suggested that we meet when you come here for a visit. Seemanti (that's her name) said she would like that very much and looked forward to it.*

Did I step into a different universe with that name? Or did you like the anonymity of our friendship so much that the first mention of a friend who wanted to meet you threatened to throw a different light on it? Other women would have thought it was the latter, other women may not have exchanged so many thoughts with you or scrutinized every word of every letter. But I am not *other women*.

When the morning sun crept up with tentative, questioning rays, I threw off my questions and decided it was the former – Seemanti. And my response is: Ah, okay. I see what happened here.

Maybe in another ten or twelve years, I will get a letter from you, picking up from where we left off! Or I may never hear from you again.

My gratitude for this brief interlude of meeting among words.

Goodbye, my dearest friend.

Love
Tara